T0299593

HERO

HERO

Katie Buckley

TINDER
PRESS

First published in Great Britain in 2025 by Tinder Press
An imprint of HEADLINE PUBLISHING GROUP

1

Cataloguing in Publication Data is available from the British Library

Hardback ISBN 978 1 0354 1307 2
Trade paperback ISBN 978 1 0354 1308 9

Typeset in Scala by Palimpsest Book Production Ltd, Falkirk, Stirlingshire

Printed and bound in Great Britain by Clays Ltd, Elcograf S.p.A.

Headline's policy is to use papers that are natural, renewable and recyclable
products and made from wood grown in well-managed forests and other controlled
sources. The logging and manufacturing processes are expected to conform to the
environmental regulations of the country of origin.

HEADLINE PUBLISHING GROUP
An Hachette UK Company
Carmelite House
50 Victoria Embankment
London EC4Y 0DZ

The authorised representative in the EEA is Hachette Ireland, 8 Castlecourt
Centre, Dublin 15, D15 XTP3, Ireland (email: info@hbgi.ie)

www.tinderpress.co.uk
www.headline.co.uk
www.hachette.co.uk

To my parents, for giving me the stories,
and to my friends, for telling me to write them down.

'The charm of young girls' irresponsibility, of their tyrannical caprices, is that everyone knows, in fact, they are fish flirting with the net.'

Mary Ellmann

Prologue

Here's how it goes. The night before you left, you asked me,
  Why don't you love me enough?
  The ring on the desk, warm from my hand. A wild, widow-making blue.

Do you remember when we used to tell each other stories before we fell asleep? You'd say, your dark curly head on my shoulder,
  Tell me a story, tell me something nice.
  They were about lost snails. Birds making friends with trees. Battles fought and ships feared gone and then come back home again, like we were kids still believing in fairy tales. You said once, at the beginning,
  Tell me the story about us. Tell me the story of you and me.
  And it was early enough that I could tell it and believe it to be true.

It isn't the beginning any more. It's today. You have been gone for a week and are coming back tonight to get your answer.

Here's how it goes.

I said, I don't think I could love you any more than I do.

If you loved me enough, you said, *you wouldn't have to think about it.*

Your bag on the floor, open and soft things spilling out of it. Laundry I had done for you and folded carefully, smoothing it with my hand the way you touch baby clothes in a store. You looked at me, wide eyed and horrified and said,

I need to get out of here,

when I took the ring off and said,

I just don't know.

I didn't believe you until I heard the zip of your bag close. I stood up then, moved as if to touch you. You took a step backwards. Bag on your shoulder like a sailor on leave. I thought, in the moment, that this was the only time since I'd known you that you'd left a room with me in it without hugging me goodbye.

I can't wait for ever, you said. *I'll be back in a week. You need to decide, Hero. This isn't fair.*

Here's how it goes.

I'll text you, I said.

And you said,

Don't.

I am not surprised that you got tired of waiting. I have been going and gone for a long time.

Where are you? you used to ask me, late at night on the balcony. My eyes on the moon.

Don't forget, you'd say, kissing me on the forehead, *to come home.*

I am going to answer you by telling you a story. Things have happened to me that you should know about. I need to tell you about things that I have done.

I am going to start at the beginning.

Here's how it goes. Once upon a time a girl and a boy fell in love. They also didn't, but when they did, the story ended. When they didn't, the girl died an old maid in a house that smelt like piss. Before she did that, they burnt her at the stake and drowned her just in case because she really was very beautiful and very odd but she grew a tail and swam away and chewed through the ropes that men use to tie themselves to masts and ate them the way you eat corn on the cob and was captured, finally, and killed and dried out and hung on the wall like those singing fish that you find in Midwestern bars. Men hang their hats on her breasts. Her scales are starting to fall off, one moonstone flake at a time. She hangs on the wall in the bar, but she is also riding a horse hard along the edge of a cliff. The wind in her hair and the sound of the waves breaking apart on the rocks down below and the fact that when we turn a couple

3

of pages, she meets the man who is going to tame her. Don't worry – when she meets the man who is going to tame her, who is gentle and kind and willing to break her in slowly the way you do with wild things, she is also making a king lose his mind with desire, launching a thousand ships, bringing down the Catholic Church in England and getting all her gowns tailored so that they show off her favourite breast (the left one). When the girl and the boy fell in love – read: I can't eat, I can't sleep, I must have you, I have ridden here all the way from my father's castle to gaze upon your loveliness – the story ended with trumpets and weeping and waltzing in a dress that changes colour in perfect time with the way he sweeps you across the floor of his father's castle.

That story ended, but another one begins, and you'd be forgiven for thinking the characters are the same – because they are – but the girl is unrecognisable. She nags and asks too much of mysterious fish and gets ugly fast and eventually dies of heartbreak when the boy, understandably, fucks his daughter's best friend. You might've seen the movie version of that one. Yes, she's a lot younger than him, but it's perfect because the story starts all over again, this time with a girl who is a girl and not a woman with a pouchy bit of skin around her lower stomach from giving birth to the boy's children. Trumpets, doves, waltzes, let's have it again from the top, but this time, with feeling. This was after, of course, the girl told him a thousand stories in a thousand nights in order to convince him not to kill her, which was brave considering how many virgins he had killed right after he fucked them. Luckily, it worked, and she was rewarded by having thirteen children in as many years and dying at forty. Luckily, it worked, and on their fiftieth anniversary, he didn't even buy her a card. Luckily, it worked, and on their wedding day, he smashed a handful of cake into her face even though she had begged him not to, and she stood there in front of everyone she knew and tried to laugh so she wouldn't cry.

Once upon a time, wedding bells, axes being sharpened, a woman falling into water with a splash that sounds like a sigh, the way to love, honour and obey has no echo to it like shouting into a cave that has no end. It's just deeper darkness all the way down.

Someone told me once that the stories we tell ourselves about ourselves are the most important stories we'll ever hear. But I don't know what the story of us is without the stories I've been told about women like me.

Let me tell you a story.

Have you heard the one about the girl who meets the boy?

Have you heard the one about the hero?

Day One

or

There were once a man
and a woman who wished very much

It was cold the day I met you. That year, autumn in the city had come on fast. The apartment where you lived with your friends was beautifully old. High ceilinged and plaster graped, the crop withering on the vine in corners of the room. The grandeur made it freezing; the landlord protested conservation area and listing when you pointed out the way the wind came through the casings at such a clip that it ruffled your hair if you sat too close to the window. My apartment, on the other side of town, was smaller but freezing too. You'd think we'd be good at cold – me with my Canadian childhood and you with your Danish mother – but only you could handle it. I slept with blankets piled up high on my bed, a reverse princess and the pea.

~

The day I met you, I was running late. I had gone to the university library after work with my waitress apron tied under my coat. The library was twenty-four hours, I had books to pick up that couldn't wait. I arrived at the dinner party when dessert – overdone brownie, the edges blackened with scorched sugar – was being served. The host didn't mind. He and I were in the early stages of sleeping together and I thought that pretty much nothing I did would make him like me more or less. I was wrong, but we'll get to that later. The only person later than me was you. You stuck your head round the door of the kitchen where everyone sat, lit by cheap, spitting candles and said,

My clothes smell like frying oil. Just give me ten seconds.

Everyone laughed because they knew you. I wanted it – to laugh with the knowing of you.

You work in a restaurant?
Yeah, I do, you said.
In the back or the front? I asked.
I feel like there's a right answer to that, you said.
No way, I laughed. It's an innocent question.
Before I answer, you have to answer a lead-in question. Do you know any chefs that you like?
Are you a chef?
Yes, you said.

I like you, I said. I was earnest. We laughed about it afterwards, how I'd said the next line. I like you a lot.

Thanks, you said. *I like you too.*

You know she ran away with someone, I heard somebody say. She eloped with a painter, they, like, left in the middle of the night.

That should have been your first warning. I was notorious, even then.

You looked at me.

Really? you asked.

I nodded.

Why?

I laughed. I took a sip of my whisky.

Why not?

An hour later and we were on the sagging, grey couch in the living room. My leg maybe touching yours.

Do you study too or . . .?

Yeah, I'm studying English, I said.

Ah, no way, me too!

I'm in the year below you, I think.

Because of the aforementioned elopement?

The very same. But that makes it sound more glamorous than it was. I'm not a sexy young divorcee – I was just away for a while, travelling.

With some guy, you said.

With some guy, I said. He was an artist, I said, as if that explained it.

You raised your eyebrows.

I was young! It was a different time.

Do you know what you want to do after you graduate? you asked.

Yeah.

I told the truth. A new decision that I was trying on for size.

I want to be a writer.

That's so cool, you said.

You?

A chef, I think. I started doing it for some extra money but I like it. I think I just like feeding people.

Fuck, I laughed, if my mum were here she'd tell me to marry you on the spot.

Good thing she isn't, you said, *given your track record.*

We don't have to run away, I said, we could be really boring and settle down here. Wait – what kind of food would you cook me?

Whatever you want. What kind of things would you write about me?

I smiled. I noticed the way your hair tumbled forward over your brow. I noticed the lightness with which you held your drink, the curve of your thumb against the glass. The freckles on your ears.

Good things, I said.

The host was your close friend. He put a hand on my shoulder.

I knew you two would get on, he said.

I don't really believe in it, you said when we were on our last drink. The red of the Campari blushing as the ice in the glass melted. Other people talking in the room. Their voices far away and comforting, the sound of strangers at the beach.

You don't believe in it?

Not really. Well, I believe people love each other. But I don't believe in that kind of 'the earth stood still and we were happy for ever' stuff.

So when people say they've felt that way, what do you think?

The shout of someone else's laughter across the room, your smile as you looked over at your friends.

I think they're lying, you said, *in order to justify all the bad that comes with it. My parents,* you continued, *say that they fell in love really quickly.*

Are they divorced?

Yeah. I can't imagine them together, being happy.

Now that I know them so well (your mother, her long rope of hair; your father who I love because he is so like you), I agree with you.

But they will have had their reasons for being together.

Sure, you said. *But they were probably the standard ones. I don't think it was this beautiful, noble thing.*

Wow, I said. A real romantic.

I know, I know, you said, rolling your eyes. *I just haven't met the right girl yet.*

Good luck to her, I said.

You kissed me on the cheek when we said goodbye and I can feel it, even now. That light singeing. A limpet, licking itself on to the face of a rock. Let me show you how important I am.

Why didn't you tell me? you asked me later.

Tell you what?

That you fancied me.

I did tell you. I flirted with you all night.

You flirted with everyone, you said, smugly. The false modesty of the winner of the race.

I liked you too much, I explained.

I thought, but did not say, that I do not believe that women like me end up with men like you.

~

I had a teacher in Fourth Grade who loved Tudor history. This was back when I still lived in Canada, back before anything happened to my dad. Before we packed up all our things in a panicked, scattering way and moved to England the year I turned sixteen. I lost things in that move that I've never found.

In Grade Four, I was being bullied by girls who all had different versions of the same sparky name. Because I was scared of bumping into them, I stayed in the classroom a lot of the time to have lunch, and the teacher would stay in there too and eat with me. He wasn't my main teacher, he was like a teaching assistant, which I guess is why he was able to spend loads of time with me and no one was too worried about it.

Why are you starting here? you'd ask me if I was reading this aloud to you.

Because this is the beginning of the myth, I'd say.

What myth? you'd ask.

Mine.

It's the first time I can remember feeling like a statue. Something dead and dumb, worshipped for those very reasons. Flowers pooling like vomit at my rooted feet.

This teacher and I, we talked about Henry VIII and his wives and how badly I wanted to be a Tudor queen. I thought it was more active than being a regular queen, but looking back on it I can see that the reason these queens seemed more interesting is because they kept getting beheaded. Violence marked them out as more exciting. I helped him organise a Tudor feast for our class. My mum made oranges spiked with cloves. I gnawed on a turkey leg next to Connor, who was dressed as a knight. He had a big coloured card helmet on, with a gold cross painted on it and paper chainmail draped over his chest. He bought me a necklace once. It was a silver chain, the kind that men wear, the kind that almost looks like a bicycle chain, and he'd put it in a blue velvet box. He stood at the edge of my desk and slid it on to the pock-marked wooden surface. He stood there with his hands clasped nervously behind his back while I opened it.

He was dressed as a knight and I was dressed as Anne Boleyn. I loved her. I was fascinated by the power that she had over a king. The teaching assistant and I talked about her a lot. I liked that people thought she was a witch because I thought that I was one, a little bit. I liked howling at the moon, which I figured made up for the fact that I didn't have an extra finger.

My dad, sister and I often went to this store called Liquidation World. They had cheap CDs, waxy candles that smelt like colours, and out-of-season holiday decorations. The women behind the counter chewed bubblegum and called me sweetie. I saw an ornamental dagger there. It was probably blunt, but it was in a sheath that had leaves etched into the tinny metal and I told my teacher about it, how my dad said it wasn't safe for children. I'll get it for you, my teacher said. Next time I'm driving down there, I'll pick it up for you. Don't tell your parents, he said.

Because I was having a hard time at school and this teacher went out of his way to be kind to me, my parents invited him over for coffee. I remember not liking it. Seeing him in my living room, laughing with my dad. Asking to borrow a DVD.

After cake, he said he wanted to go for a walk around the property. I want to see the view, he said, which was strange because it was about five o'clock and already dark. We did a sort of lip-service tour of the outside of the house and I said I was cold, and I was because it was windy, and he said, hey, why don't we go and sit in my truck?

We got in the truck and he lit a cigarette. I thought that was weird, that he would smoke in front of me with all the windows done up. I remember staring past his head at the lights of my house where I could see my parents through the window. The truck creaked in the wind. I had one of my hands on the handle of the truck door. I was so small that I had to jump into the cabin. He talked at me for a while.

You understand me better than anyone, he said. I'm closer to you than I am to my wife.

In Fourth Grade, I was nine.

I think my parents will wonder where we are, I said. I squeezed the door handle.

You don't have anything to be scared of. He was angry. We're just talking.

The wind was howling and the arbutus tree that hung over the mossbank waved her arms at me in panic.

When I was in my last year of school, a teacher implied that he wanted to sleep with me. He sat on the edge of my desk sometimes, and other times I would look up from doing work and he'd be watching me. I bumped into him once on the bus and he sat next to me and said,

I could always get another job.

I put my hand on his knee. I said,

Why don't you?

I loved it. I told that story at parties in my early twenties. I told it to you when we first met. Look how dangerous I am. Look what I have made grown men do.

Now that I'm not nine, but a grown-up woman, Catherine Howard is the one I think about the most. She was sixteen years old when she married Henry VIII. She was eighteen when he killed her. She was a handmaiden to Anne of Cleves, and her family had placed her at court because an older man was preying on her in her own household. When the man, her music teacher, started pawing at her, she was twelve. She was beheaded not for adultery, but for treason; the charge was rooted in the sexual affairs she had before her marriage, including, allegedly, the one with the music teacher.

A renowned Tudor historian described her as an empty-headed wanton. Her body was buried in an unmarked grave next to Anne Boleyn, but when they excavated the Tower, they couldn't find her. No one knows where her pretty little empty-headed body lies.

I don't think that much about how she must have felt crushed under the weight of a man whose legs leaked pus through his breeches and who had already beheaded one woman. I think about how she must have tried to make the best of it. She probably held his hand under the table.

~

I have been reading a book about self-portraits. The book is about the different kinds of self-portraits people have made and how the form has altered through time. Men's pictures are often grander versions of themselves. An exaggerated codpiece, here. A letter praising their genius, painstakingly rendered so the viewer can read it, there. Like Odysseus, describing himself as so handsome as to be godlike. Later, when the female tradition gets underway, there are lots of 'women as myth' self-portraits. My favourite is Artemisia Gentileschi painting herself as Painting, as if to say, break my fingers all you want but this is who I am.

The day after you left, I wasn't thinking about the self as myth or the self as shapes or the many women who painted their mothers into portraits with them, passing their daughters a palette or a book with a pained, hopeful smile, but the self-portrait through object, also known as the self-portrait of absence. Vincent's empty room.

A pair of boxers, thrown on to the top of the laundry basket. Your winter shoes mixed in with mine beneath the coat hooks because it's summer and you left fast. The postcard of 'Fish of the North Sea' that a friend sent you, tacked to the wall above the table. The book you bought me when we slept together for the first time. You left it on my pillow. I remember thinking how beautiful your signature was. I felt excited in this kind of back-to-school way that reminded me of all the times I sat cross-legged on the floor of the drama classroom, waiting to receive my part. It was, I know now, the feeling of beginning.

That first day without you, I didn't tell anyone. My phone buzzed constantly. My friends already knew – they had known about the ring and I think you must've told them to check on me. You loved me enough, even then, to send people to the rescue. I ignored them and went to work and polished cutlery until I could see my face in it. There was no need to look for myself in the knives.

There's a new waitress at work. She is so young but she is old enough to have dyed her hair a couple of times. Her jacket was painfully cool and when I told her I liked it, she ran her fingers over the cuffs and beamed. Her ex-boyfriend has been going round calling her a slut, she told me casually. He's saying other things about her to her friends and she wouldn't tell me what they were. But there is a new boy who's much better. He picks her up from parties, he buys her cocktails at the local bar they go to. They only go there because they don't get ID'd. Cheap twinkle lights and sticky tables. Barmen who get off on the way sixteen-year-old girls stand on their tiptoes and place their thin torsos over the bar. I used to kiss men over cold vinyl bars to get free shots. I used to wear miniskirts I couldn't walk in to go dancing.

One of the first ever proper parties I went to was in my friend's back garden in a shitty white marquee that managed to collect moss in the few hours it stood there. I had kissed a boy who I liked a lot and I was dancing, hoping that he would come and put his arm around my waist. But instead, he stood with his friends in the corner of the tent, guffawing. I drank warm, sweet cider. I wore cut-off denim shorts. I had the bruises of childhood all up my legs. One of his friends walked over and I offered my soft ear to him, thinking he would whisper something into it like,

He likes you.

But what the boy did was stick his hand down my shirt and grab my tit and squeeze it so hard that the fat disc bulged. The disco ball threw diamonds over his laughing face. He looked like a clown.

What the fuck is wrong with you? I said, when I pushed him off.

He laughed, pointed at the boy I had kissed and said,

He said I could.

When I asked the other boys in my class, boys who were my friends, what they thought about it there was a chorus of gathering doom that said:

He couldn't help himself.

We all brought tents to the party. The thing with tents is that you can't lock them. The thing with boys is that they can't help themselves. I closed my eyes when they wandered around the field screaming my name. I closed my eyes when they stood on the other side of the mesh that is designed to stop mosquitoes and other things that stick themselves into the soft parts of you.

In the end, the boy I liked crawled into my tent. He told his friends to fuck off. He ran his hands through my hair. I liked him. I thought he'd rescued me. The thing with me is, I just can't help myself.

All those same boys and I went to another party months later. The boy I liked had changed his mind and I spent hours trying to compose funny, casual texts to him. I once texted him a video of a girl spray painting in an underpass because I knew he liked his girls cool and rebellious, and said,

Hey, we should do this sometime x

Only one kiss because I was doling them out in meagre handfuls to make the coin more valuable. He read it within seconds. He never replied. But I could hear laughter in my ears and it didn't sound like mine. Something I have learnt a very hard way is that sex is a commodity that loses half its value as soon as you drive it off the lot.

At this second, loveless party, a girl got so drunk that she passed out on the couch. Some girls put a blanket over her and then we carried on. I was keeping one eye out for the boy. I wore a bra under my crop top to make myself look riper. Apple juice running down Eve's chin. I saw the boy with his friends standing around the girl who was passed out on the couch. That's nice, I thought. They're checking in on her.

The thing I remember most about what those boys did is not the way one of them asked me at school a couple of days later,

Are you still angry at me?

And it's not the way I saw them hold her head at a funny angle that only made sense when the light from the phone camera blared like a siren in her face, and it's not the way the boys scattered like flies when we asked them what they were doing. It's the way I heard them say,

What an ugly bitch,

from far away, on the dance floor.

The new boy texted her while she was at work with me. She leant over the dishwasher to show me a picture.

This is him, she said, blushing.

He's handsome, I said.

Yeah, she said.

She looked at the picture for a moment longer before clicking her screen to black.

Is he at school with you?

No, he's finished. He's nineteen.

I stopped myself from saying something about how dating older boys is better because they are more mature.

After service, we talk about the ex-boyfriend again. She talks about him quickly. It's like she can't help herself; it's like she has something stuck in the back of her throat that she needs to get out.

We could never talk about anything, she said. If he did something mean, or if I felt like he was wrong, whenever I talked about it to him, he always ended up making it—

I finished her sentence.

Your fault. He always ended up making it your fault.

I want to give her an instruction manual. I want to say, Listen, baby, for 'jailbait' see, 'Bluebeard'.

Listen, I said, I dated people like that. Pretty much everyone I've ever dated made me feel like that. You need to trust your instincts, I said. I knew it was wrong then, even though I was young. I was right.

Her phone pinged. She looked at me, hesitated for a second. And picked it up.

~

Once upon a time there was a girl who lived in a house in the woods. The house was not scary until her father died, as fathers often do in stories.

She had a swing in an arbutus tree and it flew out over a spot where the land fell away with a wistful sigh from the mountain. She took her book to the swing and curled up in the knots of rope and read, dangling over the edge of the mossbank, her dog asleep by the trunk of the tree.

She told me that she is convinced that if she went back to that forest, she would find herself there. She thinks she would catch a glimpse of herself, walking with bare feet over the wet, shaded dirt. Stooping to look at a suspicious beetle. Hair so bright that birds wheel away from it in shock.

Years passed, but not too many. The girl was taller. If she walked past you quickly, you'd think she was a woman. The planes of her face had become sharper, more granite than the sandstone galleries of youth. Her dog died. She began to feel cursed. Everything she loved, on its way out the door. His puppy collar is in a box under her bed, even now, when she is all grown up.

The girl had just broken up with a boy who had a bad habit of holding her head down so hard when she sucked him off that tears ran down her face. This boy used to lead her to a spot near the river. The ground was damp and you couldn't see the spot from the path. When she walks past it now, she averts her eyes. She doesn't want to bump into herself there.

She is in love with a man, a painter, when we catch up with her. She tells her friends she is tired of boys. She doesn't know it yet, but she will soon find out that there are so many men like this that you can spend all your time sitting in the dirty corners of their ill-decorated lives. The man says many things to her.

'How old are you?' he asks.

'What do you like to read?'

'You must be smart, huh?'

'Your hair is soft.'

'Do you like wine?'

'When did your dad die?'

'So, what is it about me that made you want to go on a date?'

'Another drink?'

'Can I kiss you?'

The girl barely sleeps. When she is without him, she can still feel the movement of his body on hers. She wakes up seasick with longing. She becomes a thief, stealing time to walk barefoot right down the middle of the road that leads to his bedroom window. It mewls when she pushes it open.

She follows that man away from the woods and falls out of touch with her friends and her family. While she is away she reads a book a day. I used to think I was relaxed, like I was always on holiday, she told me. But now I realise I was bored. I was so bored all the time.

The girl is sitting outside a bar that has tables so close to the road that you fear a motorbike will go past and smash her chair out from under her. She is reading a big, fat paperback, leaning back in her chair. Her high-heeled sandal is dangling off her foot; it rocks back and forth as she bounces her leg. Her hair is held on top of her head with an ivory pin that she bought a couple of weeks ago. Her long skirt is rucked up around the tops of her thighs and she idly fishes peanuts from a blue and white china bowl and puts them in her mouth one after the other. She periodically wipes the salt from the peanuts on her bare thigh. It glistens. The bottle of beer by her hand leaks cold and she presses it to her neck and closes her eyes.

Can't you see the way she looks at her watch? Can't you see the way she is coiled up and rippling like a big cat? We only notice these things because we saw her in the woods, remember? We watched her hanging in a sunbeam, with a big, fat paperback.

She is staying in a house from which you can smell, but not see, the ocean. You can smell and see the highway whenever you want, sirens singing down it all the time. A family live across the road and she stops to wave at the baby, who is newly walking. The room is on the top floor. The man is not there. She checks her watch again. She takes off her shoes and her sweaty feet leave prints on the black laminate floor. They disappear as she looks at them. The clothes basket is overflowing. She puts a load of laundry on. The girl lies on the bed and watches the ceiling fan rotate with muted enthusiasm. Her shadow slinks away from her on these nights when the man does not come back and the sun slides down their bedroom wall and she leans over the edge of the balcony and stares down the road. Her shadow is dancing somewhere in the city. Her shadow is slipping into the open mouth of a man who suddenly feels ravenously hungry. It slides round the corner of a house and a woman looks up from her doorway and smiles in recognition at the way the wind moans with longing.

The man says many things to her.
   'Don't call me when I'm busy.'
   'Don't interrupt me when I'm reading.'
   'You like that, don't you?'
   And the girl says,
   Yes.

The girl writes a lot in her diary. She writes things like:
   I will try to be better at asking for reassurance. I will try to be more trusting and I will try to make sure that I don't make my emotions his problem.

At night, she lies still. They don't hold each other any more. She used to hold him, but now it makes her feel foolish. It makes her feel like a barnacle, clinging blindly to a rock. If she fidgets too much he gets angry. So she lies still, watching the ceiling fan. Her hair has started to fall out. Her tongue is always dry. When she walks outside, it begins to rain. That year was particularly bad, people say to each other. That year, the rain tasted salty. She walks through knee-deep puddles in her high-heeled sandals. The insides of her pockets are always damp.

Stories like this only end one of two ways. The girl might die. Whether her body gives out is not important. She might be dead and still walking around. She might be dead and still be there in that city doing laundry and lying still. Or, the girl escapes. We all know that these are the two options. The girl, as girls often do in stories, thought there was a third option. Bluebeard changes. He realises that he has behaved badly. He stops killing women and hanging their corpses in his basement and becomes a good and kind man.

The girl escapes.

Day Two

Butch Cassidy: You know, when I was a kid, I always thought I'd grow up to be a hero.

The Sundance Kid: Well, it's too late now.

Butch Cassidy: What'd you say that for? You didn't have to say something like that.

The second day you were gone, it was beautiful here. Not a single cloud in the sky. I watched a plane, yellow light all around it. Fire from the engines maybe, some unthinkable disaster. Or is it just sunlight, tipping the edge of the plane wings? It's already autumn in the mornings and the evenings, but around midday, there is the smell of hot blackberries, unpicked and spoiling on the vine.

I texted my friends and told them I was fine, although writing down the particulars made me feel light headed. The group chat symbol is a tiny picture of a cowgirl. The horse's body is blurred. The cowgirl is in perfect focus, arched over in a backbend. Her feet on the saddle. Her hands on the round rump of the moving horse. She's beaming. I turned my phone to airplane mode before they could reply and went to work.

~

The restaurant where I work now is the best place I've ever worked. The chef makes me fishy snacks. Two prawns, bathing idly in garlic. A whelk. My mouth tastes like salt. I suck down mussels with one hand and wash forks with the other. Eartha Kitt's 'I Want to Be Evil' playing in the dining room, walking home in the dark singing it under my breath with wine bottles in the pockets of my coat.

You loved it too, when you worked here. When we'd been friends for a month, maybe more, a chef's job came up and you got it. You mainly did prep, and when I was setting up, you would often follow me around the empty space carrying half-peeled potatoes. You burnt the lemon tart cases more than once doing that – following me. The wooden floors, the empty seats. It was like a Pinter two-hander. Even more so because I was dating your friend, the one who'd hosted the dinner party, and I would go from not talking about it out of respect to talking about it in fast, anxious torrents, desperate for someone to decode him. Men never like to know about their friends' bad behaviour in case they are expected to do something about it.

Before you fuck someone you see them extremely clearly. He sat at a high table on a stool and there was something about him teetering there, sipping his warming wheat beer, that was pathetic. He asked my opinion on his politics essay and I helped him. He took me home and bent me over his bed, the window open, the moon cold and unimpressed, my beautiful red underwear around my ankles and after that we stopped talking about what I thought about things.

Why? you said once, throwing plum pits into the sink. *Why do you insist on sleeping with these guys who aren't good for you?*

What did you say? I said. I was holding a knife.

Why don't you go out with someone decent? Your standards are too low.

He's your friend! If you can find me someone actually decent I'll make sure to fuck them right away! I shouted.

It wasn't normally like that. We didn't argue often, not until we moved in together. We fucked around a lot. We had competitions to see who could split a piece of paper on the pass with the flick of a tea towel. I wrote you notes on the cheques, things like:

1 x short rib
1 x tall dark and handsome

Our friends watched us. Raised disbelieving eyebrows when we protested, said it wasn't like that with us. We were just best friends.

Before you fell in love with me I didn't know if you thought I was nice to look at or not. And I liked that. I liked that you never told me I looked good and you never pressed yourself up against me when you shouldn't have. I thought you were too good for me, and so I came to your house in big sweaters and I slept in your bed when I was drunk with my head on your shoulder. Do you remember that day when we strolled around town after we finished work for the afternoon? You sat on a chair in the restaurant lobby, watching me hold wine glasses up to the light. You said,

Surely there's something I can do to help?

And I said,

No, you sit there and look pretty.

When I finished I called to the head chef,

Have a good dinner shift. There's a coffee for you on the bar,

and we walked through the back streets of town slowly, winding our way to my apartment where we would end up sitting on my windowsill, watching people march by in the newly minted winter sun. We stopped at that café you liked, the one you took those other girls to. We got salted caramel cookies and ate them as we walked. There was a shop near my apartment that had a bright yellow painted front and a window full of jewellery and miniature silver statuettes. Pretty, mismatched plates arranged in a fan, like the ones in our kitchen now. We stood in front of it licking caramel off our fingers, and you said,

If we were together, this is what I think it would be like.

And I remember thinking,

I am not capable of calm like this.

My favourite thing about you has always been your shoulders. My second favourite thing about you is your nose. Then your hands. How they are always dirty. How your knuckles are covered in scars from where you taught yourself to cut things quickly. My first boyfriend played rugby. I would wipe blood and mud off his face and feel something twisting at the base of my skull. Then, the way you walk around as if the world is one, long, parade for you, as if every branch is waiting to be twisted into a crown for your temples. They say that you fall for people who aren't like you, but I don't think that's true. I think I fall for men who could be heroes. Cleopatra and Antony, slamming together like two heavy swords in the sunlight.

I have always been undone by the way you cook. Before I'd licked salt off your stomach and back, when we swore we were friends and I wrote your dating profile for you, I watched you separating eggs in the restaurant kitchen, the whites slipping out through your fingers. You looked at me from your place by the stove, your hair falling into your eyes and you smiled. People used to say, you must eat so well, living with him. Now, my mother tells me I've lost weight.

~

At the moment when I am sitting down to write this I have slept with 108 men. I could divide them up into lots of different categories. Men who loved me and men who didn't. Men who kissed me in public and men who didn't. But the way I like to think of them is men I cooked for and men I didn't. Most of the first quarter I didn't cook for because I was too young and I didn't know how to.

Your anxiety-inducing friend was the eightieth. I thought, that's a nice round number. I could stop here.

I cooked for him like a woman starved. He used to slump at the table in my kitchen and watch me while I made breakfast – I only ever made enough for him because I was too nervous to eat. It was a sunny winter. The light dappling the Blu Tack-stained wall of the bedroom where he slept. The slow, heady thump of a record, bodies too tired to get up to flip it. I knew I was fucked the first time I cooked for him, the first time I asked,

Do you want some toast or something? Or do you want to get going?

34

I was lying in bed with one leg out of the covers. He was in the doorway, leaning. He had come over late the night before and had carried his bike up the stairs and left it slouched in my hallway. My heart still runs hot with the tick of a bicycle wheel. The first time I saw you ride a bike was also the first night I helped you undo the buttons on your jeans.

Yeah, I could eat, he said. He smiled.

I walked slowly to the kitchen. I cracked eggs into the pan. I poured him a glass of juice. I said,

Do you take sugar?

Inches away from asking can I get you anything else? Can I do anything for you? Him, a lone guest in my starred and brutal kitchen.

I cooked for his friends as well. He would show up at the door and smile in a way that made me feel like I was going to pass out, with his friends standing behind him – you, bleary eyed and grinning with the rest of them. You were almost always drunk. You were going through a phase of drinking Baileys, like old women. It made you giggly. He would kiss me in front of the pack. He would say,

Hey, do you mind if the guys eat here?

And I would say,

No, of course not.

I lived in long dresses, his sweaters, and my mother's apron that winter, the one from the town where I was born. In that town, the forest meets the sea. In that town, the ashes of my father lie scattered in a field. I drank ice-cold white wine by the gallon. I sang. I danced in the kitchen by myself. Golden girl. See the way the sun rises for you? See how the world gets beautiful to match your mood? When I think of that winter, the word I think of is stupid. I was stupidly happy. It was stupidly perfect. There's nothing more stupid than a woman born to skip town falling in love with a boy who, like a pleasant flight attendant, knows all the exits. I couldn't run away, this time, thank God. Take me wherever you want I am a movable feast. I knew who I was this time.

One of my friends, Tex, came to dinner. She leant back in her chair, tilting so she could get a better look at us. She asked him questions.

Where was she born?

When's her birthday?

What does she want to do?

It should have been strange, but he responded to each question as if he loved knowing the answers. Afterwards, she turned her palms to the sky as if to say, see? He loves you.

He kissed me. He cleared the table. I'd made two different dinners – some of his friends were vegetarian. Me and my unfailing hospitality. I cooked them both at the same time, a glass of wine in my hand and Louis Prima on the stereo. The kitchen full of young, happy people. My friend told me later that when she went to make herself another cocktail, she found him standing at the stove eating leftovers out of the pan. His big shoulders stooped in the light of the extraction fan. Licking cream off the spatula.

Fuck, he said. She's such a good cook.

He cooked for me once. He made pancakes. Not just for me, his perpetual friends were all heaped around the kitchen table like soggy cardboard cut-outs of themselves. I sat there in one of his big T-shirts and a pair of black knickers that his cum was seeping through, and ate in delicate cat-like bites. I laughed when they laughed. I said funny, bite-sized things. When he broke up with me because he didn't want a girlfriend, just the full service that came with one, I didn't say anything at all. I kissed him goodbye, I opened my mouth to speak and he smirked and said,

What? You want one more time?

But he gave me a book, which I still have on our bookcase. He gave me something he loved and I simplified the fraction.

I sent him something I had written about him once. He texted me in the middle of the night, saying how he couldn't
stop
thinking
about
the things we used to do together. Not me. The things. I sent him something I'd written, which is almost exactly

37

the same as someone asking if they can fuck you and you saying, yes of course, and while we're at it, do you have a section of your floor covered with glass that we could do it on? He messaged me back and said,

That's beautiful. It's so us.

I danced down the street the next day. Giddy with joy. Palms raised to the sky. He loves you. He called me that night, I was so happy. He asked me to take my shirt off and I said,

I miss you.

When I took my shirt off, he said it back.

~

I used to think that being a waitress was glamorous. You'd watch me stuffing tips in my pockets and ask,

Is that all for you?

when I counted the notes out with the practised rapidity of a bank teller.

I'd buy everyone drinks and there was a night where I drank Guinness and shots of whisky to impress you. What is a woman but a fiction? Who am I, but a myth? Now, all the bones in my bad foot click when I take my shoes off. I pick glass out of my hands over the kitchen sink. My clothes smell like beer. The word 'slut' comes from the word 'slattern', which used to mean both a kitchen

38

maid and a hussy. So when you say, isn't she such a slut, you can mean isn't she a dab hand with the scourer and doesn't she look like she loves choking on cock. In the mid-fifteenth century, when the two meanings started to blur together, I'm sure men looked at their maids scrubbing on their hands and knees and found the word incredibly useful.

I read *Tess of the D'Urbervilles* when I was sixteen as part of my A levels. Everyone made fun of a girl in my class because she wouldn't shut up about how much she related to every gorgeous and maligned heroine, from Curley's wife to Becky Sharp. This girl loved *Tess of the D'Urbervilles*. She talked in class about how Tess was so beautiful and so misunderstood, and I remember leaning back in my chair and rolling my eyes. My friend, laughing under his breath. When I was sixteen I thought Tess was a moron. I hated her. Not because she was beautiful – I'm beautiful, so I understand what it must have felt like to dance through the village and feel the weight of glory shaking like bells around your body. I hated her because she was stupid. I hated her because she didn't have a shred of interiority or common sense. I hated her because she didn't think that naming the baby Sorrow might not end so well. I hated her for falling in love with a man named Angel. I hated the way she collapsed out of one disaster into another like a person trying to navigate one of those reality TV obstacle courses. I was smart. I was sixteen. Things like that were not going to happen to me because I could think my way out of them.

I was at a dinner party once, before I knew you, and there was a boy there who I thought I loved. He was the poshest boy I'd ever considered dating. He wore pressed shirts to university every day and wanted to work in something he never bothered explaining to me. Business, etc. He was obsessed with me until he got to know me. At this dinner party, we were already essentially over and I was not being cool about it, but I was trying. I didn't talk to him very much. I laughed at other people's jokes and later that night I fucked someone else. But before that, I went up to him and said,

Hey.

I'd been making cocktails for everyone all night, and when I said hello to him, he said,

Yeah, I'd love another one, thanks, and put his empty cocktail glass in my hand.

No one writes books about waitresses. Everyone wants to fuck the waitress but no one wants to write about her, which is surprising, given the male literary penchant for putting words in the mouths of women you don't listen to. There is, however, a famous Manet painting of a woman standing behind a bar. She's listening to a man talk and one of the reasons the painting is so famous is because the expression we see is one of complete and utter boredom. Her face is tired. Her eyebrows are slightly raised.

What? her face says.

But in the mirror behind her, there is a different version of that barmaid, who leans over the bar, her body saying, what? Tell me what you want and I'll give it to you.

My first job was working evenings after school at an Italian restaurant and I made five pounds an hour. The manager ran his hand across the bottom of my back whenever he moved past me. I told my boyfriend, a painter who spent his Saturday nights smoking cigarettes in the bathtub in his mother's house while I was on all fours scrubbing rat shit out of the walk-in fridge, about the manager touching me. When I met that particular boyfriend, I thought he was cool in a way I have outgrown so fast that it bleeds to walk again in those shoes.

He said,

Ignore him. He's a loser.

So I did and I worked until I lost ten pounds from running around and eating nothing but chicken salad, taking as many shifts as I could because I was saving up to run away with the painter. I can cut pizza perfectly now. I can throw dough up in the air and catch it on my fingertips. What a little slut.

That boss fired a girl because she complained about the chefs sexually harassing her.

Yeah, he said, maybe they were. Or maybe it was her perception.

Amazing, isn't it, how far perception will get you.

When we were friends I told you I'd had bosses who tried to hurt me. You looked at me with your big dark eyes. We were walking through the park in the cold. Frost, sparkling with pleasure at the closeness of you. Me, doing the same thing. Your friend and I had broken up and you were dating a girl with a lisp that made your stomach flip over. It was nice. I miss it sometimes, being your friend. This road is the one-way kind. When I told you, you stopped walking in the middle of the pavement. Your breath like a happy steam train. You put your gloved hand out and I put mine into it and we kept walking, four feet on an endless bed of worthless diamonds. You asked me where you should take that girl on your next date and that was that. But you held my hand for the rest of the walk.

When I first got to uni, I needed a job desperately. I had signed a lease I couldn't afford; my student finance didn't even cover my rent. I got a job at the first place I applied and felt lucky. The food wasn't great and I never got a break. I would eat cold chips in hurried, greedy handfuls, wiping my oily hands on my thighs as I ran back up the stairs from the kitchen. But the customers were friendly. A book club met there every Monday night and I would linger while I cleared their plates, trying to catch a glimpse of the cover. Hoping I had read it too and if I had, trying to figure out how to drop that into conversation. My boss was in his fifties. He slunk. He complimented me on how tidy the tables were. He would wrap his fingers around my hip and say,

You look good today, sweetie.

He started to organise the shift patterns so that he and I worked together, alone. The kitchen was downstairs so there was no one else around. Just customers waiting to be served. One night, cleaning and yawning with my palm over my mouth, I hoovered with one hand. He said,

Two hands, you stupid bitch.

And I jumped and said,

Sorry.

Eyes automatically on the floor.

That same week he told me that I didn't get to keep my tips because we didn't know each other well enough yet. I watched him putting twenty-pound notes people had pushed into my hands in his pockets. I thought of the books I had to buy for my course. Expensive men. Hardy and his poverty-stricken temptress. I watched him turn the tip jar upside down so he could get three fingers inside it instead of two. His nails scraped the glass trying to get the last coins out.

Another day. A lunch shift. I had already cried once, sweeping the mezzanine floor. I had pushed the fat of my palms into my cheeks as if to drive the tears back into my eyes. Crumbs on the hardwood. The sound of him pacing below me. The neon-blue light of the sonic mouse deterrent winking at me and screaming quietly. Pests too big to sweep up. Holes too small to fit into. I went downstairs. I whistled, shakily, under my breath. I was bending over a table to light a candle and I felt him come up behind me and rest himself on my thigh. He leant over. My body almost flat against the table my skin centimetres from the candle in its pretty glass holder. Have you ever seen a rabbit about to be speared by a hawk? They press themselves against the ground so hard that their spines go convex. They almost break themselves trying to be small. It never works. He reached his horrifically long arms around me and brushed his thumbs across my breasts. The chefs' laughter crashing into the stainless-steel kitchen surfaces and ricocheting up the stairs. His breath smelt like coffee when he said,

You should be careful. If I want to fuck someone I do it. I don't ask. I just do it.

I worked the rest of that shift. I don't know how. I laughed at customers' jokes for the next six hours. I wiped tables. I cleared up broken glass and told the person who'd broken it not to worry and that it happened all the time.

I went back to work the next day and the day after that for weeks. The other waitresses smiled at me in a way that meant,

   I'm worried about you,

   whenever I clocked on and they clocked off, relieved laughter following them out of the door.

I left in the middle of winter. I got a bursary and I quit my job the same day. My best friend and I went for margaritas. I licked salt off the rim and grinned the smile of a rabbit who outruns a hawk.

A few months later, I was walking to the library and a car slowed beside me. My hair was up in a jaunty ponytail, tied with a ribbon. I was whistling. The car crawled on its belly next to me and I looked in the window with a smile, not knowing who was in it and when I caught his eye his lips curled back over his teeth. And I kept on walking with my books clasped hard to my chest.

~

My mother left school at sixteen because her parents needed her to start working. She keeps her Head Girl pin in a box next to her bed. She tells me how she once punched a girl for disturbing her when she was studying. In hindsight, a useless fight.

   My mother, saying,

I'm not clever enough to read your dissertation, darling.

My mother at sixteen, a skinny tomboy. On her bike on her way to the library.

~

After I got my bursary, I spent most of my time reading and laughing. I got sky-high grades. I wore them under my clothes like beautiful lingerie that nobody else needed to see.

Another thing I did when I got my bursary was extra-curriculars. I joined the Literature Society and edited the short-story submissions. I bought a long, square-shouldered coat to wear to meetings. One of our most promising young poets had grabbed me at a mixer and I sat on the desk with my legs crossed in my serious coat and my teeny-weeny skirt. All the boys loved that I was clever because it turned them on to watch me purse my lips at a girl rambling about something and cut in with,

I think we're getting a little off topic here.

But it didn't turn them on when I disagreed with them about what we should publish or made them look bad, and so when I rejected a story on the grounds that it was breath-takingly misogynistic (inspired, the cover letter admitted, by the work of John Updike) they overruled me and made me meet up with the guy who wrote it to apologise and tell

him we were publishing it after all. The poet who kissed
me said something about professionalism and being
respectful to people on the other side of the aisle, as if he
were a politician, and I thought about reminding him that
he had to be pulled off me by multiple people when he
crushed me up against the wall at the mixer. He screamed
at a woman who told him to leave me alone. A nightmare
circus, coloured disco lights on his face. Women around
me shouting.

I decided it might be unprofessional to bring this up.

I didn't let Updike junior pay for my coffee. I paid for his
and bought myself a cookie, which I broke up and ate slowly
while he talked. We didn't talk about writing at all. He said,
    You look beautiful today.
    He invited me to a party.
    He said,
    What kind of thing do you normally wear to parties?
    He said,
    You looked amazing at the social. Wear something like
that. It'll be good for my flatmates. They need to meet
different kinds of girls. It will be illuminating for them.
    I laughed.
    He said,
    Let's go for a walk.
    I put on my professional coat. We had been walking for

ten minutes when he pointed at an enormous Georgian building and said,

Oh, how funny, that's my house.

It had big, dead-eyed windows.

Do you want to come in for a cup of tea? he asked.

And I said,

No thanks, I've got work in an hour.

I clipped away in my best boots, hands deep in my pockets. I could feel him watching me walk away and I had to breathe through my nose to stop myself from running. We published the story and I left the Literature Society.

Months later, I bumped into him on a night out and he put his arm around my bare waist, the fleshy weight of it making the chain I had looped above my hips bite their little gold-plated teeth into my skin and I had to breathe through my nose to stop myself from being sick.

~

My friends and I, we have this fantasy. We're bandits in the Wild West. We're called the Mustang Maidens and we're notorious. We each have nicknames that people can't bring themselves to say out loud in case it will conjure us up. The saloon door flying open. Four silhouettes outlined by the dusty sun. In this fantasy, everyone is scared of us. We run the town. We get the loot. Spurs dripping with blood. The ominous, too-close laughter of women who know what you did.

Even though we are bandits and we are quite busy doing that, we still have day jobs. People have their suspicions, but even if anyone knows that the laundry maid at the Hotel Rio Bravo is also one of the four Maidens, the one with two guns, the one they call Two Shot because she'll shoot you twice to be sure, they don't even whisper about it. The men think about whispering. Sometimes they edge around it, like vultures dancing around an almost-corpse. They stand on porches made of wood that seem parched, as if the trees are desperate for water even now, after they've been hacked up and put back together. Sure, it's strange that a couple of the girls around here aren't married, and sure, we saw the primary teacher shoot a hawk out of the sky without even looking, which is damn-near impossible. She heard the hawk scream and she shot it with her gun in one hand and that put the fear of God into every man in this town, but she is a good teacher. And pretty too. Pretty enough to make you think about leaning in the doorway of the schoolhouse to watch the curve of her arm when she writes

A   B   C

on the board in white, flaky chalk. You don't, though. Can't risk it, with a body that much bigger than a hawk.

The Maidens have a reputation for stealing, of course. They wouldn't be good bandits if they played by the rules.

There isn't anyone can hold a candle to them in terms of looting, and they aren't polite about it, which disappoints some folks.

You'd think, an old timer says, if ladies were gonna steal our jobs they'd at least be nice about it.

The thing with the Maidens is they do other things too. A man who beats his wife is found in separate pieces, nailed to the fence that borders the town. They never find his beating hand. That bit stays missing. Overnight, all the women in the town seem to have guns and seem to know how to shoot them. A man who likes to dish money out to his wife in feeble, chicken-feed handfuls, finds that she stops asking him and is wearing a new, red blouse.

Where in the hell did you get that? he asks her.

She doesn't answer. She polishes the mother-of-pearl inlay on her rifle.

I'm a barmaid. That's my day job. My nickname is Quick Fingers, and Two Shot and I do a bit where someone asks,

Why's she called Quick Fingers?

And Two Shot says,

Well, (raising a glass of whisky, boots up on the table, this conversation always takes place right before a shoot-out), you either be rude enough or nice enough to her and you'll find out.

I'm known for being sharp as a whip. Men throw silly insults at me and I slap them away with a look or a laugh that makes them sit up a little straighter. A forest fire making everyone put out their matches a touch more carefully. But there's something fun about forest fires, isn't there? Something new. There's always some idiot who decides to flick their lighter open and press my cheek against it. There's always some guy who tries to push me back into heat. In real life, I have been burnt many times. I have roared into flame only to be tenderised from the inside out. In that town with the Maidens and the rotting body parts of a man who never should have looked me in the eye when he bragged about the way he hit his wife methodically, one side of her face and then the other, always with his right hand, the same hand he uses to pinch my ass when I come out from behind the bar to wipe a table, I never even get singed. We win, every time.

That barmaid, the men say, chewing.

She is smart, my God. You see the way she hauled Johnny over the coals? Jesus Christ (tobacco hitting the bottom of a copper spittoon).

Scares the shit out of me, one of them says.

I like it, from a younger, softer one. There's something sexy about it.

The other men hush him; they're sitting in my bar, after all. And there I am, wiping glasses and smiling and making one of the old men laugh. I'm giving him another glass of amber on the house. I have red boots on. My favourites, because blood don't show on them. I'm sweeping my gold-rush hair over one shoulder. I'm going to empty the tip jar into my pockets later, like I do every night. My boss doesn't question it. He knows I deserve it. And do you know what my signature phrase is, as a barmaid in a town called One Shoe, or Lonely Ridge? Do you know what I say when some moron gets mouthy and asks me how much for an hour upstairs? I get my gun from under the bar and I say to every man in there,

Put your hands where I can see them.

~

You're still polishing? Two Shot said when she walked in the door. The people in the dining room paused in their conversation. I wanted them to leave and gave them the bill half an hour before, which they picked up idly from time to time.

Give it to me, she said, holding out her hand for the tea towel.

Babe, it's fine, I'm almost done.

I'm not fucking around, Hero.

The steam from the wine bucket full of boiling water and vinegar smelt brown. It clings, like sea air, to the hair and skin. When the hero comes home, people ask him how he got his scars. How can you do that, a boy asked me once, watching me pluck a teabag out of a mug with my bare hands.

I've burnt all the skin off my fingers from carrying hot plates, I said. I can't really feel heat any more.

You should become a thief, he said. No fingerprints.

Just let her help you, The Kid said, or we'll be here all night.

Two Shot pulled a chair out with her foot.

Sit down.

Oh my God, I said. I'm not dying. I'm fine.

People who are doing well, Tex said, do not listen to Norah Jones.

This is a fantastic album.

It's sad, she said, and you're sad and that is why we're here and that is why you aren't allowed to do any more work.

I get paid to work here. You bozos don't. All you do is show up and drink.

Ooooo, said The Kid, standing on a stool, one hand on the good tequila that lives on the top shelf, I'm Hero and I like to suffer. Will they notice if we drink this? She held up the gold-topped bottle.

Yes, I said. But they won't mind.

There was a sound. Slightly raised voices. The refined clatter of silverware on hardwood. You never know. Last week, a customer was so intent on paying that he pushed me into the wall to stop me from handing the card machine to his friend. I only noticed my hand was shaking when I put it on the chef's chest to stop him from causing a scene.

You guys OK in here? I said.

There was a teaspoon on the ground, encrusted with chocolate and now, flecks of dirt. The girl, younger than me, stared at the table. The man was texting. I recognised him, had recognised him when he sat down. He plays golf on the green outside the restaurant. He is old enough to be her father. The chefs and me sometimes play 'Boyfriend or Dad'. You often can't tell until the open-mouth kissing starts. A hand on the knee? Dad stuff. An innocuous little, my baby only drinks white wine? Easily could be dad stuff, not that I'm an expert. I recognise him, I realised, as I was kneeling down to pick up the lost cutlery, because once he pissed outside the restaurant against a tree that you can clearly see from the big windows. I made eye contact with him as he walked up to it. He looked at me and smiled as he handled his soft, small cock out of his imitation tweed trousers.

I picked the spoon up and put it in my apron pocket.

Can I call you a taxi or anything?

No, it's OK. We're going, I think, she said.

Sure, I said. Well, I'm here if you need anything.

When they leave, I resist the urge to put my hand on her wrist and whisper,

Be careful,

in her ear.

I resist the urge to stick my foot out as he leaves to watch him smash his face against the door handle. Maybe the chrome edge of it would hit his eye socket. Make jelly. Women are good at that, right? I want to lean over his prone, oozing frame, and say something that ends with, capiche? Instead, we all watch them leave and we watch her trot along two steps behind him in her too-high heels. What a silly dress. What a silly girl for thinking it matters how nice she looks.

Well, Two Shot said, when the door closed behind them, that was fucking depressing.

He was gross, Tex said, wrinkling her nose.

Aren't they all? I said.

OK, where is your phone? I cannot take any more Norah.

Tex held her hand out and I sighed and pulled it from my pocket.

Ice? The Kid asked.

Please, I said.

Is this, I asked, the *Dirty Dancing* soundtrack?

Yes, Tex said, I can't stop listening to it. I went to *Dirty Dancing Live* last week and it was all hen dos and then just me and my mum. And all these women were going berserk, like fully screaming every time the boy playing Patrick Swayze came on stage.

Was he hot? The Kid asked.

Meh. He just made me want to look at Patrick Swayze.

Been there, I said, raising my glass in a toast.

But they were screaming and then, before I knew it, I was screaming too. I was rabid.

And your mum? The Kid asked.

Practically frothing at the mouth.

Wow, Two Shot said. Glad to hear the divorce hasn't blunted her instincts.

Husbands come and go. Patrick is for ever.

Well, I said, he did die. Of – they are rolling their eyes – cancer.

Jesus, Two Shot said, you are determined to be miserable.

I am not! He did die of cancer! That is a fact and I am allowed to know sad facts.

I have a sad fact, Tex said. She has her boots up on the counter. They're green snakeskin.

Oh God, not you as well, The Kid said.

My sad fact, Tex continued, is that I had the best sex of my life yesterday with a circus performer.

There is a pause.

What? I said, incredulous. How is that a sad fact?

It isn't, Tex said. I was just desperate to tell you and didn't know how to successfully move the conversation on from people who've died of cancer to fucking an acrobat.

I hate you, Two Shot said. Where do you meet these men?

I met him at a club and then I had sex with him.

She makes it sound so easy, Two Shot said, neatly folding the tea towel. Where does this go?

Oh, just shove it in the big blue laundry bag.

Ah, thank you, she said.

Her belt buckle is a bronze bull head. I know she has cigarettes and mints in her bag. In mine, I have a knife she bought me. It has bees carved into the handle. For my queen, she said, when she gave it to me.

So, I said, what made the sex so good?

Tex looked at me.

Well, I think it probably has something to do with the fact that he's a circus performer.

My favourite line from any movie ever is from *Butch Cassidy and the Sundance Kid*. The Kid is sitting in a dark cottage, alone, playing with his gun. A young woman comes in – it is her small cabin, we realise – and it is a few seconds before she sees him, sitting there in the shadows. She jumps. He says something like,

Take it off, and gestures at her dress with his gun. He does this until she is in her petticoat. He goes over to her and reaches into her corset. She says,

Do you know what I wish?
What? he drawls.
And she says,
That once you'd get here on time.

Do you think, I asked, that you've ever really, honestly
been yourself around a man? The way we are with
each other? The way we are now?

If men heard us talk like this they wouldn't believe it,
said Tex. They would see it as something we were doing
for effect. They would think it was totally for their benefit.

Yeah, The Kid said, if you took away all the parts of
my personality that were for a male audience I don't
know how much I'd have left.

The table, strewn with cigarette boxes, empty tequila glasses.
The way I walk in long, regal strides. To define yourself
against something is to still be defined by that thing.

Being a woman, I said, is like being in a badly written
novel and the author is some self-styled *enfant terrible*
who says provocative things about the state of the
nation and penises.

Or indeed, Tex said, the state of the nation's penises.

I could write a book on that, Two Shot said.

I should hope so, said The Kid, all that research
you've been doing.

~

I can think of two honest interactions I've had with men. Strangely, they were both on a holiday me and Two Shot took when we were twenty-one. We were so young and I lost my phone on the first day, had it stolen by a beautiful man who asked me for a lighter on the beach at 4 a.m. and I waved him over to my bag and he took everything except my wallet, which I thought was unusually kind.

We ate a lot of things heavy in fat that left a film on our lips and coated the inside of our mouths. That summer in Barcelona, I continued, we played a game where if we liked something – a wine, a view, a plan, the first bite of chocolate fudge cake, warm from sitting in a glass case in the window – we would moan loudly like porn stars. I think, I said, we were making fun of the silliness of choreographed sex. We spoke often in those days about how ridiculous it was in porn when a woman would scream and cry out at the smallest touch (on the inner thigh, the cheek, the elbow). But I think we were also so happy and we wanted to loudly express our pleasure, turning something artificial into something honest. It was, of course, also very stupid and sometimes resulted in men following us down the street. Men followed us down the street anyway, so we thought, I suppose, that we may as well have some fun before our painful and inevitable deaths. We ate almost every night at a tapas place called El Xampanyet, a bar known for there always being standing-room only due to the fact that there weren't any seats and you whistled and shouted to the waiters to get served plates of things in oil and things in cream. By the end of the holiday the waiters called us Las Meninas.

Remember how they handed us bottles of house cava whenever we walked through the door? Two Shot said.
    I remember.

A friend of my sister's lived there. She was engaged to her now-husband, a painfully handsome Italian man who I looked at for too long. Nothing bad happened – I had already paid the tax, via the lost phone – and we flirted a little and drank spritz in the cool eddies of the old stone city wall. They had a neat, elegant flat and I was jealous of their life, but in the way small girls are jealous of women in their early twenties. It was undercut by the belief that it would eventually come to me too: it was a natural progression for me to end up with a beautiful life. We ate carbonara, the fiancé carved thin, acorn-scented slices of ham from a leg on a stand in his living room, and I got so stoned that I fell asleep under their coffee table.

We went to the beach with the girl, her fiancé, and
their friends. A beach, she said, only the locals went
to, and it was quieter than the beaches we had been
visiting, no English tourists playing music out of
tinny speakers. We had graduated, part of this cosmopolitan gang already, and we drank Campari and white
wine from small plastic cups. Their friends were all
men (another sign of high status I coveted), most of
them Italian and Russian, and a couple of impossibly
smooth-chested Americans who played frisbee with
us and seemed flustered by our decision to play
topless, the sand stinging my breast when I dove into
the dunes, catching the disc in mid-air. After frisbee,
I was tired and lay on my side, listening to the others
talk and admiring the sharp curve of my waist to my
hip, the dramatic topography of it. One of the Russian
men asked me if I was too hot. His hair was blond
and cut so tight and neat around his ears that a line
of pale, newly exposed skin showed through around
his hairline, like a little boy with a new haircut for
back to school. I said I was too hot. He took an ice
cube out of the coolbox, laid it on top of my hip,
holding it between two fingers, and ran it slowly up
and down my flank. He didn't look at me once, he
looked at the ice cube the whole time. It was so
refreshing that I closed my eyes and when I opened
them his friend, one of the American boys, emboldened

by the Russian's forwardness, was doing it too. They were playing, letting go of the ice cubes and watching them run away down my side, trying to knock the other person's off, replacing each cube when they had melted into nothing and become spots of damp on my beach towel. I talked to the others and napped and they kept playing, using my body as a board for their new game, almost like air hockey, but also cooling me down. I'm sure they must have known how good it felt, the shock of the cold blue against the white heat of the sun. It wasn't sexual or platonic, it was something charged in between, helped I think by the fact that they only touched me with their fingers when they lost control of their cubes and needed to scoop them up quickly or rescue them from some shaded hollow, like my hipbone or the small of my back.

A couple of days later, we were sitting outside a bar on a back road that was quiet, it being too early for dinner and everyone still asleep or just waking up in the cool-faced shuttered apartment buildings. We were sun drunk and sipping our cava, which in those days was one euro fifty a glass, watching the bubbles file cheerfully to the surface like small children being led outside to play. The sun fell in huge, hard-boundaried blocks of light that carved the road into a kind of hopscotch, alternating squares of heat and cold that could be leapt through. I was – we were – very young, but something that stands out to me now is how we knew we were. We felt young on that trip, which is at odds with how I felt in much of my late adolescence and early twenties – always straining to be older. Everything mothers ever say about getting older is true. It is a blessing that we only ever live through each decade once – twenty on repeat would lose the thrill, the sharp taste of yourself on someone else's fingers. But it's a shame that you never get to use all the things you learnt about being twenty again. That must be why mothers impress these things on you so earnestly. It is enraging to be told that you are heartbroken because you are nineteen, not because he was the love of your life, and then suddenly you are talking to your best friend's little sister, telling her that the reason that she is heartbroken is because she is nineteen. On this evening, though, I was aware of how new everything was. Maybe that's why, when the men came and spoke to us, we turned them down as a matter of course, almost without thinking, as if we were suddenly aware of our vulnerability.

I've regretted it ever since. I don't know about you, I said, looking at Two Shot. The men, there were two of them, one sandy blond and freckled, and the other dark and chiselled, striding up to our table and smiling in a way that made me smile too. They asked us how we were and how we liked Barcelona. They were German and so spoke in a delightful singsong that made them seem very soft, and after the niceties were exchanged, one of them said look, we think you are very beautiful and we'd like you to come to our apartment tonight and have sex with us.

I laughed and you – I gestured to Two Shot – always more practical, asked what the intended pairing up would look like, and they shook their heads and one of them said, oh no, you've misunderstood, it would be a – uh – group sex thing, and I was charmed by how he didn't dress it up at all. They gave us the address of their apartment and said they hoped they would see us later and then they left, looking back at us once, still smiling. We decided instantly not to go in the name of safety, but in retrospect, I think it would have been fine. I think their lack of guile was honest and really quite refreshing. I liked it, in the same way I liked the ice cube game. It felt, for a moment, as though sex and bodies could be entered into in a casual way, as just another thing to do on a sunny evening. Maybe fucking them would have disenfranchised me of this fantasy, but I don't think so. I think it would have been nice.

A group of men walked past, leering through the window. One of them tried the restaurant door, making us jump.

Thank God that's locked, The Kid said.

It was fear that stopped me. I hate that, I said. The way it robs you of the freedom to believe it will be different.

I don't know, Two Shot said. I worry that it would have been bad, with those guys.

They seemed like nice guys, I said.

The whine of blood in my temples. Sweat between my legs. Where are you? Are you drunk with your friends too?

But the issue is, Two Shot said, good men are still men.

~

What's the worst sex you've ever had? I asked Tex.

She has a tattoo of a fish between her shoulder blades. One of my favourite things about her is her ability to escape, to wriggle herself off the hook. She used to leave dinner parties earlier than everyone else so she could go home and read the paper in the bath.

It wasn't sex, Tex said. I wouldn't describe it like that.

What killed me, she said, was how, when I saw him the next day, he said hi and how he'd had fun the night before. As if it had all been normal. And I was standing there on the pavement collapsing in on myself. My great-aunt told me a story once about how she had these beautiful peaches that she grew every year. Every year she made cobbler and pie and jelly and lovely salads with thin slices of these golden, sweet peaches in them. One year, she noticed how many wasps there were that summer. They were a nuisance and she made trap jars of orange juice, the rim lined with blue cheese to lure them in. They like the smell of rot mixed with sweetness. But for every wasp she caught there seemed to be another; she couldn't get rid of them. Still, the peaches grew. She could see the orchard out of her kitchen window and she waited until they looked perfect to pick. She went out there, one August morning, with her basket and a straw hat, to harvest them. The first peach she grabbed crumpled in her hand. She turned it over and found a small hole, with impossibly tiny bite marks lining the edge. She crushed the empty shell in her hand and went to grab another. The same thing. They had all been hollowed out from the inside, but had hung, still glowing orange, as if nothing had changed. It was the wasps, who had crawled inside each peach and eaten all of the fruit from the inside out. She was sad about the loss of the pies and the jellies. But what she couldn't get her head around was the malice of these little things. Why let her wait all summer, thinking all was well? Why let them hang there so perfect? She would have, she knew, done something if she had seen the destruction that was happening right in front of her. But she couldn't see it. And that's how they took them all, every single peach.

Tex breathes in.

And that's how I felt, how I feel when I think about it. Like an empty peach, being crushed in the palm of someone's hand.

~

We're outnumbered! I cry, looking round the corner of the woodshed. My fingers held in a gun. My small, embroidered waistcoat covered with pine needles. Dirt on my knees. My sister, playing today the role of the law, skulking through the trees. My father, like me, is a cowboy.

How will we escape? I ask. My father crawls on his knees, swears under his breath.

They're everywhere, he says. He pretends to put bullets into his blue plastic gun.

But what will we do? There's law to the west, the east, the north, the . . . I frown, forgetting the last one.

The south, my dad says. They've got us all right.

My sister giggles from behind a tree.

Take some bullets, he says, holding out an empty hand.
I put them in my gun.

Listen, partner, my dad says, when we get out there, I
need you to do one thing.

Yeah? I say.

He says, his eyes green to my blue, pines hanging over
the ocean,

Stay low and keep shooting.

~

It is a couple of hours later that The Kid says,

So when are we going to talk about what's actually
happening?

Not tonight, I said. We aren't at that part of the story
yet.

Early on in our friendship, you and I talked about writing
one night after work. Sitting on the grey, exhausted couch
in your old flat.

Do you ever write about your life? you asked me. We were
sharing a bottle of beer and passing your phone back and
forth, taking turns to play songs.

Yeah, I said. I pretty much only write about myself.

I'd love to read some of it, you said. *Your writing.*

Oh, I said, I don't think you'd like it. I don't think it
really sounds like me.

How's that?

Well, I would say that I'm quite a happy person. But my writing is pretty angry, as a rule.

Did you tell me I was sexy when I'm mad? Or was that someone else?

Maybe I'll switch up the vibe and write about you, I said.
Yeah? you said, smiling. *Why?*
Because, I said, taking a deep breath of the cold air, you're the best man I've ever met.

My mother says that even when you show men who you are they don't believe you until it affects them and then they go wild. Turned Frankenstein by the desire to remove the parts of you that are not convenient.

~

There was a young man who loved a witch. These were not the days of witch-hunting. No one was accused of witchcraft in this town for the simple and convenient reason that all the witches had been killed hundreds of years ago. Of course, some men were scared of women who walked with pride, but it rarely led to public executions. Murder was committed privately, often at home. But these murders were different from the grand killings of the past. The mayor was never present. You couldn't take the kids to watch.

A word on this young man. He did not believe in love. He did not believe it ever happened. He laughed at his friends as they tumbled into the abyss one by one. He said, boldly,

Love is a chemical reaction in your brain.

He said this at the dinner party where he met the witch. She wore a black dress, cut low. She came through the door carrying a bag of wine and said,

Sorry I'm late, we had a lunch booking that overran and I had loads of cleaning to do.

The plates had been cleared away when the conversation turned to love. She drank whisky. When she asked for it, three men stood up to get it and her friend said,

Christ, guys, at least pretend to be cool.

The witch was leaning back in her seat with her stocking-clad feet propped up on the chair next to her.

Love is a chemical reaction in your brain, he said, when someone asked him what he thought. She frowned. She stuck her finger in her whisky to stir the ice and then licked it, looking at him. I'm sure she has an opinion on that, someone said, gesturing to the witch.

Why? someone else asked.

She ran away with someone when she was younger. She eloped.

You did? he asked.

I did, she said.

That's so exciting, a girl sighed across the table.

The witch smiled.

Why? he asked.

Why not?

People saw them laughing helplessly together on the grey sand beach and said to each other, how did she manage it? She must have done a deal with the devil to get a man like that, the women said, watching the witch hanging out his boxers on the line with her hair all mussed up like he had just released it from his hand.

The torches outside her house by the crossroads burning all through the night. Moans coming out through the open windows.

Are you really a witch? he asked her.

Yes, she said.

What can you do?

I can tell that something is going to happen before it does.

Like prophecies? he asked, propping himself up on one elbow in bed to look down at her.

Like prophecies. But it's only for bad things. I only know when bad things are going to happen.

How do you know? he asked.

I ask the moon, she said.

One morning, some months after he had moved his things into the stone cottage and put his boots by the front door, the witch got up and got dressed in the dark. The front door whined. People dreamt of gates when she walked past. They dreamt of mazes and tides and losing something important. Of going down into the belly of the earth and looking for it. A woman woke up as the witch walked past the window and curled her arm around her husband's stomach, whispering,

I dreamt you'd died, in his ear.

The witch walked to the edge of the cliff that jutted out like a proud chin over the judgemental ocean. She stood, facing the water. She raised her palms to the sky. She asked the moon a question. But when she walked home the moon began to repeat the question over and over again.

Perhaps, she thought, I have brought this on myself by believing in my greatness. I have brought this on myself by wanting everything too much.

And the moon whispered, does he love me? Does he love me? Does he love me does he love me does he

The witch felt despair sitting outside her front door like a three-headed dog. The moon poured through the window and woke the man. He got up in the middle of the night and drew the curtains and when he got back into bed, he pressed his cold feet between her warm ones. She whispered in her sleep.

Does he love me? Does he love me? Does he?
  And he thought, do I?

When he left her, the witch kept living. We may suspect, in fact, that she cannot die. She consoled herself with the fact that, at least, she saw it coming.

Day Three

or

Old, New, Borrowed, Blue

Why don't you love me enough?

I do, I said, I do love you enough.

It was so hot this summer that people haemorrhaged out of town like blood after a bullet to the stomach. We bought iced coffees and sat on the top deck of the bus. You pointed out places to me that you went to as a kid. The bend in the river where your dad persuaded you a crocodile lived, and the bagel place he took you to after, where he'd pick you up to set you on the chrome stool and wipe mustard off your chin. We wandered around the deserted jewellery district, the pavement channelling heat up to the back of my knees. You pointed at a sea-blue ring in a shop window.

Do you like that one? you asked.

Yeah, I said, I love that.

We looked at each other and I slipped my hand under

the back of your T-shirt so I could touch your skin. The shop owner watched us walk away. Wondered, maybe, why we didn't come in.

~

I told you the legend of my parents one night when you stayed behind to help me mop. You probably didn't ask me to tell you a story, but I remember it that way.

Tell me a story. Tell me something nice.

Isn't it funny how we go back to draw the lines? To make 'you were made for me' feel more true. What is

you were made for me

but a mistranslation of

I own you.

Your parents broke up when you were little. I think, looking back on it, even then I was talking you into something. It can work, you know, I was saying.

When my parents first met, my mum was living with a man she was sure she wanted to marry. They lived in a beautiful, red-brick cottage, in the part of the English countryside that is particularly known for growing rapeseed. He did not want to marry her, which is maybe why she longed for it the way she did. My parents fell in love quickly. My mum kept her diary from the year they met and there is a page that has their first date noted down and you turn four pages and it says 'Getting married.' My father used to leave mixtapes on my mother's front doorstep. They were begging to be caught. We still listen to the tapes now. We smile at the way 'James Taylor – Your Smiling Face' looks in my father's spidery handwriting. We smile at the fact that a big strong man sat down and wrote 'Baby Can I Hold You' on a small strip of lined paper. He must have tucked it into the case gently so he didn't crinkle it.

After they had been in love for a short while, my father said,

I'm moving away, and I think you should come.

I don't know where it happened, or when, but I imagine this conversation taking place in a pub. The low, easy voices of other people drifting past their table. The smell of hops and the laughter of men. My mother, leaning back against the wall. My father, leaning over the table in a suit jacket, his sleeves riding up to show his white cuffs and a watch that my mum wears sometimes, even though it is too big for her and clunks around her wrist like a hand-cuff. He said,

I'm leaving tomorrow. I'm taking the train to the airport. If you aren't at the station at

(I don't know what time it was, maybe eleven)

eleven, then I'll go and that will be that.

Mum has never told me what she thought, or what she said, or what she felt. Back then she wore black skirt suits and had long nails that she painted red. I want to go back and slouch in my cowboy boots in the corner of the pub. I want to watch her, leaning against the wood-panelled wall with her legs crossed under the table and one, patent-clad foot resting on the top of my father's fawn-coloured brogue. She looks at the ceiling when he stands up to get them another drink. She cannot see the sky, the roof is in the way, but she knows it is a shade of blue that looks like victory.

The first time you told me that you loved me, I laughed. Maybe not out loud, maybe not in this version, but one of me laughed as she watched you sit on the edge of my bed with your skater cap crushed in your balled-up hands. We had been friends for a year. I had slept with somebody else the night before, a man who worked in a small, clean fish-monger and who didn't make me feel anything when he walked into the room. When you walked into the room, I felt relief. I had always felt that way about you.

I think I love you.

And I said,

OK, how long have you felt like this?

Since we kissed, I guess. I thought it wasn't a big deal, but it is. I had to tell you, you said.

Thank you for telling me, I said.

I rubbed your back as if you were sick. The other version of me stood there and laughed. She couldn't believe her luck. So she didn't.

You talked about me to your friends, dissecting the details of my texts until they were exasperated. They begged you to give up. You drank too much. You ordered cocktails with tiny umbrellas in them and cried about me to Hawaiian-shirted barmen. You said, what's happened to me? Haunted, that look on your face. Our friends talk about you now as a die-hard romantic. But back then it gave you whiplash that almost broke your neck – all that belief all at once. A cartoon anvil bedecked with wildflowers, falling directly on to your head.

Later, I said,

I can't just be someone you fuck at university. Either this needs to be serious, or you should leave me alone.

I assumed it would scare you off. I assumed that even if you were desperate to sleep with me, you wouldn't risk being expected to commit to me. I was gambling big in a high-stakes game. I cared so much what you thought about me because you seemed to like me for my personality. The next day, you called me.

I deleted all the dating apps on my phone, you said.

OK?

What I'm saying is, let's go for it.

~

Before Apollo spat in Cassandra's mouth she must have felt lucky. All that beauty and all that knowledge and a god who lies at your feet and writhes with want. When Cassandra was dragged from Athena's temple and raped on the steps of it, she must have looked up at the sky and thought, no. I am one of the lucky ones. I am beautiful and smart and people have loved me. Dragged from the temple. Staring at the sky, which watches you with a shade of blue that looks like apathy. The wind blowing your quick heartbroken breaths away.

The man my mother lived with, the one she left for my father, sent her letters when she ran away. She still has them but she can't read them because they're too sad. They are kept in a pastel papier mâché chest that sits in the cavity of her bedside table. The letters from him mingle with letters from my father, Mother's Day cards that I made in elementary school that say things like, 'My Mum loves crisps. My Mum hates doing housework' in a six-year-old's scrawl. He proposed to her as soon as she said she was leaving. He begged her not to go but you cannot argue with a suitcase in the hall or with a woman who has realised that love is not an option, she has no choice. She tells me that she used to wear Minnie Mouse boxer shorts to bed, like a twenty-five-year-old. She used to drive around the countryside in her red sports car with her red nails, singing along to mixtapes made for her by my father, who loved her.

The man went away for a weekend once, with some friends who didn't like my mum. The man went without her, even though he expected my mum to be polite to these friends when they came over, and to look after his children, even though that isn't relevant to this story. She made the most of it. But, that weekend, she couldn't believe it. A version of her begged him not to leave when he drove away in his tasteful Mercedes, leaving her in her Minnie Mouse boxer shorts in the gravel driveway. She went back inside. She walked around the house and looked at the pictures of his children on the walls. She stood still for a moment in the hallway, biting her lip. Then she called her girlfriends. They came over, they drank his port and ate his cheese and laughed all evening, sitting on the grown-up rug in front of the grown-up fireplace. When they ran out of firewood, my mother went outside to the woodshed that leant against the red brick of the house. She took the hatchet that was wedged tip first into the chopping block and she walked calmly back through the kitchen door and chopped up his antique furniture to feed her fire.

A train is pulling into the station where my father is standing. He has a briefcase in one hand and a newspaper in the other. It is early autumn, and the smell of hot rails mixes with the almost cool air of a September morning. He has a light, long coat on. I see him from a distance, partly because I cannot remember the exact features of his face any more. The train is there, at the platform. He hesitates. He looks up and down the dull brown brick concourse and squares his shoulders in his coat. He checks his watch. He looks up at the blue sky.

My mother is running down the stairs in her black patent shoes and her black skirt suit and a long coat like my father's, which flies out behind her, and when she gets to the bottom of the steps, she stops. She looks up and down the concourse and she sees him, standing there, by the open door of the carriage. He turns and sees her. He smiles with relief and puts his briefcase down in a square patch of triumphant autumn sunlight so he can catch her as she throws herself into him.

When my father died, my mum must have looked up at the sky and thought, no. I am one of the lucky ones. I have already escaped. He brings me flowers for no reason. He cries when he listens to Tracy Chapman because it makes him think of me.

I look like my father. I have the kind of bone structure that suits chainmail. When I was growing up, people always used to say how much I was like Mum, but I think that's because we carry ourselves similarly. We wave in the same strange way – one hand reached out, the fingers clasping thin air again and again instead of moving from side to side. I have grown into my father's face, perhaps by necessity. He was never going to submit to disappearing all in one go. His personality set up encampments on the edge of my brow. My smile has been colonised by his own. His temper is written across the set of my lips.

My father proposed to my mother casually. They were crossing the road in the city they had run away to. It was winter. Light was hitting the water of the harbour and violently bouncing off it, so that my mother had to shield her eyes with her hand, even though she was wearing delicious eighties sunglasses that obscured most of her delicate face. My father put his hand on the small of her back as they crossed the road. He was almost a foot taller than her. They often went out for dinner at a Mexican restaurant down the street. They went there the night before they got married and ate tacos and drank beer and held hands. But on the day that he proposed, they were just walking home. Running errands. Their feet hitting the ground at the same time. A shopping list in the pocket of my mum's jeans and mints in the pocket of my father's. The crossing was still beeping when my father said, not even looking at her, looking at the traffic that he would stop if it threatened to crush her,

I think we should get married.

The rush coming right as she stepped off the road and on to the raised pavement. That perfect lift.

I told you this story. You did it exactly the same way.

He wasn't looking at her, but he was smiling. He knew she would say yes and she did in the same relaxed tone, as if they were just talking about whether or not they should watch a movie or whether they needed eggs.

~

The man that I left for you – the fishmonger – was sure that he did not want to marry me. But he was very kind. He had brown eyes – almost black – and when he took me on walks I would think how like the large, rough rocks that scattered the landscape they were. Dark and nice to rest on when your feet get tired. He gave me plastic tubs of samphire, bright green and coiled up like sleeping snakes. He never asked me to do anything. He brought me tea in bed and glasses of wine in his large bath. The tiles decorated with brightly coloured aquatic creatures, a hangover from somebody's childhood. He washed me once, using a red plastic cup to pour water down my back and over my head. I felt so tired all the time – working too much, studying too hard – and he would show up and put me in his car and take me out for a cheap Italian dinner or on a walk by the sea.

We talked about it often, how we weren't in love. About how the people we thought we were supposed to have ended up with had moved away or left us. He was still in love with an ex-girlfriend who should've been long gone but still hurt, the part of the splinter that festers out of reach. She called him on our first date. He stared at the phone where it lay next to the cheese and charcuterie board. It buzzed on the upcycled wood of the table and he stared at it. He looked at me, sitting across from him in a lace-up leather top, looking like madness poured into a mould, and he swept his finger across the screen and rejected the call. It hurt him to do it. You could tell by the way he leant back in his chair, collapsing into it like he'd been running from something that was right behind him for miles. I knew that when I left the next morning he would lie in bed for a heart-staggering beat before he rolled over, grabbed his phone and called her.

I would kiss him in front of customers at his work, leaning over glass cases of fish, mouths open in shock at their new miserable situation, as if I meant something by it. We went on long walks. He'd drive me to the beach because I love the sea and we'd have rock-throwing competitions, like a couple of kids. His cheeks flushed the same colour as the late evening sun and I would look at him sometimes and think, maybe. I would curl up in the front seat of his warm car and pass him the flask of coffee that we were sharing and feel safe and think that this was what it was like when you got older. This is what you ended up wanting. After you told me you loved me I sat on his couch and drank his wine. My feet were resting in his lap.

How would you feel if we stopped seeing each other? I asked.

I think that I would feel OK. It's never been that serious with us, he said.

Yeah. Like, I love hanging out with you, but . . . I don't

think I feel the way I should if we're going to keep hanging out.

We'd been sleeping together for a while. His record player
– inherited from an uncle – was playing Louis Jordan's 'Is
You Is or Is You Ain't My Baby'. The dark green leaves of
his houseplants shivered lightly by the open window. It was
raining a little, and cars drove slowly on the street below,
their tyres hushing each other on the wet pavement.

When I walk into a room, how do you feel? I asked him.
He took a sip of his wine. He shrugged. Exactly, I said.
And when your ex walked into a room, you felt fucking
elated, right?

He nodded.

The story of me and this kind man I thought about loving
goes as stories like this tend to go. It writes itself around
you while you stand in the middle of it, crying or laughing,
depending on what part you've been assigned. When I
started to back away slowly, sleepwalking from nights with
you, he noticed. He changed his mind. Wanting me
desperately because I was pulling on my boots and smelt
like pine-scented wind coming through an open truck
window. The way he looked at me was different. His brow
softened. One of the times I went to the beach with him,
he walked ten steps behind me with his hands in the
pockets of his loose grey jacket like I was a queen. Strong
boots treading gently on to water-logged sand. The sunset

falling over itself to get closer to me. The long, winding drive home with my hand on his knee an imitation of happiness.

I last saw him six months after you and I started dating. We sat in a pub that we had gone to many times before. The bartenders were used to seeing us together. I put my hand on his canvas-clad arm and asked him how he was, and he leant back against the red leather and asked how you were. It is, after all, a small city. There was, in the end, some overlap between the two of you. Marks on my body that he noted and did not comment on while we wrestled the thing between us to the ground.

He's good, I said.

Yeah? he asked.

He was looking at me so hard it hurt. And I had to explain that I loved you, that we were in love. I spared him the details.

So what about your plans? he asked.

What do you mean? I said.

I thought you wanted to, like, travel and write your book. That's why we were never serious.

I frowned. I decided not to bring up the ex-girlfriend (they're back together now, of course).

Well . . . I started.

He tried to kiss me and I recoiled in disgust, thinking of you. He wiped tears off his face with his sleeve and laughed at himself the way that you do when you know it's hopeless. The barman tried not to look at us. I've never been back to the pub, fearful of being struck by a delayed onset of guilt when I saw the faded leather of the seats. Him asking,

Are you sure?

The weight of his hand on my knee. Caring about him and the way he drew little circles on my jeans with his thumb too much to make him move it.

We played cards there once, me and him. He won every hand. I was flushed with laughter and whisky. An old man leant over and said,

Lucky in cards, eh? Unlucky in love.

I've always found it funny that love stories end when people get together. Sleeping Beauty and her prince, dancing over the credits. Ariel, giving up her tail. What happens next? I want to know what happens to them. Butterflies keep getting trapped in our house and I am sure that they are doing it in an effort to tell me things that I don't want to know. I turn my nose up at them as they flutter around the kitchen with their blue and pink wings like sugar icing on an enchanted cake. I herd them like a shepherdess with particularly erratic charges. I used to think that if I ran hard enough my feet would lift off the ground and I'd be able to fly. I used to think that sleeping with boys would make them like me more. I used to wish to meet a man as handsome as Prince Eric and I used to wish to be a mermaid and not see the problem with wishing both of those wishes. The butterflies keep coming into the house and then leaving, and I can't fly. A magpie has taken to sitting on the balcony rail. There is mould creeping into the house, growing blackly in the corners of the ceiling. The world is pouring omens over me and I am being drowned in signification.

~

I knew I loved you when I sat on a bus driving away from you and listened to Dean Martin all the way home. I listened to 'That's Amore' unironically. I laid my head back against the scratchy blue and yellow fabric of the head rest. I drank cans of lukewarm beer and thought about the way we had woken up three hours before in my bedroom. Already kissing. My phone pinged and before I looked at it, I was smiling because I knew it would be you and I was right. When I walked in my mother's front door, she took one look at me and said,

What's wrong?

It was your birthday a week after I left him for good and told you I loved you back for the first time. We went on a trip to the coast to celebrate. Throwing our things in the back of the car like bank robbers. We made terrible packing choices that we laughed at when we unpacked the car a couple of hours later.

Why, I asked, holding up a sequinned minidress, did I bring this?

You made me wear it to the pub for dinner. It was silent. It was an old fishing pub, with pictures of boats on the walls. The table was covered in little dents and a sign above it said:

'THE LADIES DANCED: THESE TABLES HAVE AUTHENTIC STILETTO MARKS'.

Our room above the pub smelt like damp and there were enormous spiders in the shower. Waves hitting the rock beach just across the road. You slept with your arm and your leg over me. You brushed my hair to help me fall asleep. I dreamt of long journeys coming to an end. I dreamt of home, the door always unlocked and you always inside. And I dreamt of fire. A city burning to the ground, and me, throwing the matches as I ran in the other direction.

Do you remember when we saw that train on your birthday? We saw an empty train sailing across the landscape of wind-blown green wheat a little after 11 a.m. The car had to stop to let it pass at one of those red-painted wooden crossings that seem minute, making you feel like a tiny toy person by association. It sang past us completely empty. But I felt that if I had looked harder, I would have seen us on the train. My hair, held up by a red ribbon. A thin white blouse hanging off my shoulders and you, laughing at something I have said. Two long coats lying abandoned on a seat nearby. I see us everywhere. All the beautiful empty things are full of you.

I remember thinking, I am one of the lucky ones.

~

On the morning of the third day, my sister called me.

I have something to say.

Yeah? I said, frowning. Pain behind my temples and the taste of wine stuck in the back of my throat. I could hear the baby in the background, sucking.

He's the nicest guy you've ever dated. And I would be so angry if you two broke up. He's a catch – you don't want to lose him.

Right, I said.

What have you been arguing about? she asked me.

What we always argue about, I said. He thinks he's always right and I hate being told what to do.

Good relationships are about compromise, she said. You need to let him tell you what to do some of the time.

Sounds fun.

Life isn't about having fun. I'm coming up to see you this afternoon, OK?

Honestly, babe, I'm fine—

I'm bringing the baby and food for your fridge.

I have food in my fridge.

I'll be there in, like, three hours.

Great, I said.

Hero, it's so messy in here, my sister said when she came through the door. She put the baby down on the floor and then immediately picked her up again.

This apartment is not baby proof.

That's because, I said, I do not have a baby.

You could have one in here if you wanted to.

This is a studio apartment, I said. Where would the baby sleep? In the bath? On the balcony?

It could sleep with you, she said.

I'm not ready to have a baby, I said, my voice rising. I have other things to do.

Like what? she asked.

Like write a book and travel and – I don't know – go out and explore and do things.

You can do those things with a kid, she said.

I think it's pretty difficult to write a book with a small child in the house.

Either way, she said, you have to get married before you even think about having a baby.

Oh my God, I said, who said I was thinking about having a baby?

We're going to need a bigger apartment when we have kids, I said.

It was our first Christmas living together. We'd put up our tree. We lay underneath it afterwards, the way I did when I was little, to look at the lights from underneath. When it was that cold in the apartment, I would put my feet between your knees in the night. You never complained. You sometimes went under the covers and rubbed them between your hands.

Oh yeah, you said. *We'll need a nursery.*

I looked at you from where I was writing: at the kitchen counter, my knees pressed against the washing machine.

No – I said – I'll need an office. With a door that locks.

Do you want kids? The Kid asked me at a party. I was sitting on the kitchen counter watching her make us fresh drinks. All the sound from the party muffled, like we were underwater. I had left you dancing, having fun. Thirsty after screaming along to 'Before He Cheats', knowing you never would.

Yeah, I said.

Me too, she said.

It's a tough one, though, huh? I said. She passed me a drink. I stirred my whisky with my finger to help the ice placate it.

She's powerful. She wears soft coats while she does important things. She has a job so big it would never fit in my studio apartment.

He wants kids, doesn't he? she said, gesturing with her head to the room where you were.

He's desperate for them, I said. But not yet. I can't see myself staying home all day with a baby and becoming the kind of person who has a practical haircut and who has school-gate friends. I know I'm being mean, I said.

The trouble is, she said, I don't think anyone can. It still happens to you. You have a baby and you get boring.

My mother tells me about her great-aunt. She had thirteen children.

Her husband, my mother says, wouldn't stay off her.

She died at forty.

Do you think she wanted to have thirteen children? I ask.

My mother shrugs.

What else was she going to do?

My sister passed my niece to me. She twisted my gold Athena necklace around her fist, as if she was trying to break it off. I laid my cheek softly on the top of her fragile head.

Please can we not do this right now? I said. I'm really not in the mood.

I just don't understand, she said, why you would let him go. After all the jerks you've dated. Think about what happened when you were away. That almost killed you.

You lost like half your body weight and cried every day for a year. You want to go through that again?

I don't say anything. I look out the window. I am not surprised to see a solitary magpie staring in at me. Last night, I drunkenly left out raisins for it. Inviting sorrow in to play.

Sit down, she said. I'll make you a cup of tea.

I can make it, I said.

Hero. Just, sit down.

Fine, I said. There are cookies in the jar.

We're having scones. I brought them from home.

~

For years, I dreamt about getting married. I used to be one of those women who suspect a proposal every time their partner takes them out on a nice date. It's so degrading, that guessing game. I used to wish for it until the painter said, drinking a vermouth at a rooftop bar, the twinkle lights swinging in the wind that always came before the rain,

If you want to make me feel sick, talk about marriage.

I hadn't even been talking about us. I'd been talking about his defeated friends who were finally starting to hang up their scuffed skater shoes and shuffle meekly down the aisle reeking of IPA.

That's messed up, you'd said, when I told you about this. *I can't imagine being with you and not wanting to marry you.*

Here's how it goes – the night that he fucked me for the first time, I was wearing underwear purchased out of my allowance. Did I ever tell you that?

My mother says of this episode,
    You couldn't be told.

In ancient times, the old men say, girls were stupid like they are now. Some things are true no matter the century. The past is thin and can be dissolved on the tongue. It feels like it happened yesterday. Time runs over me, I am a pebble at the bottom of a furious river. It was 2012, it was 1512, it was 1012, it makes no difference. This is a myth. The moral of the story remains grimly unmoved: your father at his father's funeral.

A couple of noteworthy points: he wanted to be a painter and isn't one, and I wanted to be a writer. His eyes were the brown of a still body of water when the silt at the bottom has been disturbed by a bare foot or a fish. I am tall and I came up to his shoulder. A tattoo of a mountain on his ankle, a relic from a trip he took before I knew him and when I was still in school. His head shaved so close that the contours of his skull were visible, the tremors under those tectonic plates sending emergency after emergency to my coastline. The other details aren't important. Where I first saw him. What his weight felt like the first time it sank on to me. Things that used to be burnt into my mind, branded so deep that the edges of the wound still weep in certain kinds of weather.

In one version of this story, he's a painter. In an older version, he's a knight. He could hold a sword although I never saw him use it, he rode in a way that made you jealous of the horse, and when he looked at me I considered hurling myself into the path of a crossbow arrow just for the joy of him saying,

Thanks, baby,

as I bled out in some mud in some place where he was the only person who knew my name. I gave him my sword and knelt at his feet. Bowing in worship looks exactly the same as kneeling to be executed. Catherine Howard and I. On our knees in front of the king.

Now, I don't understand how he managed to make it feel like my idea. Him kissing me up against a wall. His hand under my shirt. His cock pressed against my thigh.

You, he said, breathing hard, are going to get me into trouble.

This is a fiction – an old one. You know how it starts and you know how it ends. We can play a game of fill in the blanks.

When I think about that time it is all in hot, dark flashes. Like something you see out of the corner of your eye. Like something you know would be wet to the touch. Sitting on his lap in a damp and seeping field by the river. My push-up bra around my neck and his hand in my jeans. Painting my nails silver and thinking, as I looked at my fingers braced against the wall next to his bed, that they made me feel like an astronaut.

This is a myth and I hoped it had changed until I met up with a friend's young sister. We talked about her boyfriend. A wanderer, she called him and I thought, yes, I know the type. I managed not to say anything until she said,

I'm sure deep down he finds me attractive.

And I said,

Deep down? You're twenty years old and you think this guy who's taking a break from work to find himself and graduated college when you were eleven thinks you're attractive deep down?

She looked at the table. She has dark hair that waves down to her waist, a walking talking Rossetti. She is smarter than I ever was and we used to take her to parties when she was fourteen and watch her sip a single beer for hours. Before we talked about the boyfriend, we talked about the next election, Ana Mendieta, how much we both love her sister.

I said,

I'm not going to be able to give you objective advice. But I can tell you a story.

Here's how it goes.

In that time where I followed him around, we had a lot of conversations about things he wanted to do. He had opinions on topics so widely varied that I thought of him as a real Renaissance man. He never did anything. Even on this trip, this big adventure, he just talked. When I was that young, I confused it with ambition.

Do you ever wonder, The Kid asked me once, what his friends really thought about all of it? I mean, he was older than we are now.

I wonder that all the time, I said. I don't think anybody thought it was weird, but maybe there were conversations that went on that I knew nothing about.

Especially his female friends, right? she said. Surely they must've been uncomfortable.

I don't know, I said. I remember them asking me about our sex life. We were late to dinner once and I had red knees from carpet burn. And they laughed about it. It's weird, I said, when I read our messages back, he talks about art all the time. It was like he owned everything. Nothing I knew was worth knowing.

Everything was arbitrated by him. But he was, I said, just some guy. If he asked me out now, I would laugh. I would look at his skinny jeans and his half-finished paintings and I would laugh.

Nobody was surprised that he was older than me. Not even my mother, who loved him at the start. You were always, people told me, going to end up with an older man. You are a handful. I wasn't surprised either. It felt fated, me and this man who read difficult books (*Shantaram* and Murakami), talked about politics and sex, and was so grown up that we didn't need labels, we were too mature for that. We needed to live in the moment, which meant never ask about the future, never question him, never show want or need. I recognise it now – the oldest trick in this book. He will love you more the less you demand. Be everything and nothing. Learn how to take it without gagging. Say thank you afterwards. Say thank you when he calls you on time. Say nothing when he doesn't. Boys my age were child's play in comparison.

I reread our messages periodically to check that I am not crazy. When we were apart, I often wouldn't hear from him for days. I sent him heavily filtered pictures of myself lying pouting on the bed to remind him that I existed. He often chose not to dignify them with a response.

He says things like,

> Don't bring up your sexual past around me. It makes
> me uncomfortable.

I had so little of a sexual past that I still looked up blowjob
tips in *Cosmopolitan*, desperate to get it right.

He says things like,

> I shouldn't have to tell you I love you. Your insecurities
> are not my problem.

It would almost be funny if I didn't reply to all of those
messages in the same simpering way. I said of course,
don't worry, I understand. And I ended almost all the
messages with
   You're my hero.

He was hesitant about parts of it. That's how I remember
it. He didn't ask me to come with him, I volunteered. He
made sure I didn't get too comfortable, stressed that he
wanted me to have my own life, that he hated the feeling
of someone waiting at home for him. We talked a lot about
his needy ex-girlfriends. He was the kind of man who
hated to be thought badly of, but didn't let this colour his

decision-making – not thinking badly of him was another kind of labour he outsourced.

I remember sitting opposite him at some bar in one of the dozens of cities we passed through. My hair was so long. A river of sunshine that dripped down my back and ran off in falls at my hips. The air was hot and I'd probably had a beer. I drank a lot then. We were talking about something so inconsequential that I can't even remember it now, maybe it was where we wanted to eat or whether we would leave our passports at the hotel or take them with us. I'd enraged him somehow, earlier in the day and now I sat across from him, curled up tight in my seat. All of my effort going into keeping my face blank.

I found my journal from those years. The pages are warped from heat and pool water and bus tickets stuck carefully down. Hearts drawn around their borders, the pen pressed in hard. I lied to myself constantly. It's the strangest feeling, reading lies you have written only for yourself. I must have been so desperate to believe something different. In this city where he barely spoke to me but slid into my body every night on thin, cold hostel beds, I wrote,

I didn't know it was possible to be in love like this. I feel so lucky.

Little hearts all around. You can feel how hard I drew

them. They have dented the paper. I know that feeling still. If it is written down then it must be true.

He shouted at me that night, in the bar. He shouted at me for talking too quietly. Can you imagine? He calmly shaved my heels down, leaving bloody strips of skin on the floor all around us like ghastly vegetable peel and then took a step back and decided I wasn't tall enough. I remember walking down the road ahead of him that day and trying to figure out if I could leave right then. I remember looking into cars as they sped past and trying to find the strength to raise up my arm to flag one down. Later that night, when he and I went out to dinner, we forgot to close our window and left the light on. I wore a new sundress. A string of shells hung across my throat. Flames, murmuring under my feet. When we got back, the slanted ceiling of the room was covered in a twitching carpet of butterflies and moths, like something out of a nightmare. He was beside himself with worry about the insects and tried to rescue them all one by one. It seems to me now a spectacular display of cruelty. He was capable of gentleness. He chose not to be gentle with me.

He would probably tell this story differently.

When people starve to death, the stomach consumes itself, desperate for nourishment. I missed him when he was there and wandered around in a stupor when he wasn't, walking directly into traffic and barely flinching when tour buses blazed past. I closed my eyes like a cat and pushed myself into his hand when he touched me. Afterwards, it seemed perverse. I felt it all on my own.

You write, someone says to me, like you have something to prove. It isn't about winning.

I close my eyes. I hear the whine of a blade, singing through the air. I go back in time. I kill him. I burn his city down.

I love you, I say, as I am falling asleep.

I never asked him why he took me with him if he didn't love me. I know the answer now. What was I but a warped and shimmering mirror at a fair, fun because it makes you look taller than you are.

He shakes me awake. He says,

Why don't I have a clean shirt?

He underestimates me. It is the last mistake he ever makes. I pretend to give in. We part amicably. He sees me pull away from the shore. When I sharpen my knives, I think about him, refusing to try a cake I spent five hours making. I think of him, telling me to get out of the car, and leaving me on the side of the road. I think of him, dancing with another girl at a party, her even younger than me, me stood in the corner in my heels and my new dress, eyes shining like glass on the top of an unfriendly wall whenever the light hit them. Him saying, I can't be bothered to deal with this right now, when I brought it up, and me saying, I'm sorry I'm sorry I'm sorry I'm sorry I'm

In his version, I'm a minor figure. It's different in mine. I wipe my knives clean on my jeans. I pick up my pen. Another roadside case of he said, she said.

I looked at his Instagram yesterday and there was a new picture. The first since we broke up years ago. And it looks like I could have taken it. He looks exactly the same as he always did. He's wearing the same T-shirt, drinking the same drink. Smiling in that same old lazy way. I actually wondered if I had taken it and he was posting a photo from when he was young and I was younger. But I realised, after reeling for a second from the possibility, that that was insane, the photo must be new. It's that nothing has changed. He is exactly the same as he was when we broke up. You couldn't make that mistake with me. I look at the camera differently now. I used to look like I had just been told to smile.

A normal night in a hotel. He was on his phone. I was sitting on the floor pasting receipts and tickets into my journal. The night before, I had slept down there. He'd complained that I hadn't shaved and I had a rare flash of anger. I wasn't a teenager any more. I was starting to sense that something was wrong. But I doubted myself. He hadn't spoken to me since.

Do you love me? I asked.

He looked up.

Why would you fucking ask me that? he said.

I started crying.

Why do you always need reassurance from me? Jesus Christ.

He stood up, stepped over me. I leant out of his way with my arms wrapped around my legs, still sitting on the floor, the cold linoleum pressing against the skin spilling out from my denim hotpants while he grabbed his keys from the bedside table and shoved his wallet roughly into the pocket of his grey distressed jeans. Before he left, he said,

When I first met you I thought you were this independent woman. You act like you're so confident and smart, but you aren't.

This is a myth. Let me fill you in on a little secret: he never changes and all the blank spaces are me.

Near the end, I sat at a bar with him and his friends, listening to them talk about philosophy. I was dreaming about libraries, the clack of keyboards. The feeling of a scarf, rubbing my cheek in the wind and walking into warm pubs, friends grouped around tables. It all came true. Books scattered around my room at university. They made me feel safe, when I woke up and saw them in the middle of the night. But then, none of it had happened yet, and when they started talking about utilitarianism and I contradicted one of them, my boyfriend laid his hand on my knee and said,

Stop,

under his breath.

The guy I disagreed with had gone to Harvard and jerked his head when I spoke, a bobblehead on a dashboard. He said,

Let me explain the trolley problem to you—

And I said,

I know the fucking trolley problem. It's the most famous pop philosophy thought experiment of all time. The point I'm making is that consequences matter.

My boyfriend said,

You don't know what you're talking about.

I was drunk on sangria, and whenever I got drunk enough I experienced doses of adrenaline that made me stand up for myself, although I always regretted it the next day, and he said,

You're embarrassing me and I'm doing you a favour. If I was embarrassing myself – a smile on his face that meant he thought himself incapable of being as base as me – I'd want you to say something.

I poured my wine down his shirt and left the bar.

I never want to forget any of it. I want to keep it all, in case I need reminding why I carry a sword.

~

I love being married, my sister said, handing me a cup of tea.

The baby found your old toy shark and kissed its snout over and over again. I almost took a picture to show you.

Mum loved being married, she said.

I don't know that that's true, I said, smearing jam on a scone. The apartment was hot, even with the windows open.

She loved Dad so much, she said reproachfully.

Loving Dad and loving being married are not the same thing.

I guess, she said. She has grown her hair long and it swishes near her waist. She is skinnier than I am and taller. We used to joke that she looks like Legolas – something elfin and fast.

Remember when we used to play druids in the forest behind the house? I asked.

God, she said, we were such weird little kids.

We used to bury all the dead animals we found and then we'd, like, draw murals of them on the walls of our treehouse.

She grimaced.

You used to make me go into the treehouse first to sweep up all the spiders.

Yeah, I said. I got scared more than you did, like when that whale swam under the boat and I was so convinced it was going to swallow us that I sat below deck and just sobbed.

Dad shouldn't have let you watch *Jaws*. I touched it, she said.

I know – I was so jealous. What did it feel like?

Kind of like a wet tyre.

Gross, I laughed.

Remember when we built that raft out of Styrofoam at the marina? she said.

Yeah, of course I remember. When I fell off you stood me under the hand-dryer in the bathroom in my underwear to try and dry me off before Dad caught you.

Oh my God, I forgot about that, she said, covering her mouth with her hand. You lied to Dad and said you'd jumped in so I wouldn't get in trouble.

He believed me as well, I said. I was such a little shit.

She held out the plate with the scones. I shook my head.

Hero, you need to eat more.

I am eating!

All you have in your fridge are pickles and a weird amount of mayonnaise. You look pale. You used to look so healthy.

Thanks, babe, I said, rolling my eyes.

The baby brought me the shark. She held it near my face.

She wants you to kiss it too.

Oh, right, I said. I kissed it. The baby giggled and marched away, satisfied, the shark throttled in one hand.

What is it about being married that you like? I said.

A lot of things, she said. I like that I don't have to make plans to see my husband. I like that he's just there, all the time, whenever I come home. There's something about it, she said, that makes life easier. Like, there's all this stuff I don't have to think about any more, all these decisions that I don't have to make by myself. I like that everything is always a duet, kind of. Even if it's just what we're having for dinner or what colour we should choose for curtains in the baby's room. I love that we do all of that thinking together.

In the past, she said, I wanted that with other people, but I felt like I was always convincing them to want it too. My boyfriend before was always on the verge of breaking up with me. I think I talked him out of ending it maybe two or three times. For our one-year anniversary, we went to Paris together. We rented bikes even though I hated cycling and we went around the city and he talked at me about Toulouse-Lautrec and Flaubert, and often cycled so fast ahead of me that I would lose him and cry, alone in the traffic. We went out for this fancy meal one night at a restaurant that I had found and booked. The restaurant was really beautiful, with all these old mirrors hanging on the wall with gold writing on them, and red leather chairs, and rows and rows of bottles behind the bar. It was like walking into the 1930s. I wore this little black dress I had with a fringe at the bottom and I felt so beautiful, like I was in a movie or something. I kept waiting for him to say something, to notice the effort I'd made. I remember sitting there expectantly and then the feeling of realising that he wasn't going to compliment me sinking in and getting embarrassed about how short the dress was and how much makeup I was wearing. He couldn't really afford it and I spent the whole meal worried about the awkward moment of when the bill came and whether he would let me pay for it or he'd insist on paying and then sulk about it for the rest of the trip. I had this like, disappointed, nauseous feeling because it seemed like it was going to be so perfect and magical and then it wasn't, you know?

I know, I said.

Thinking that every time I had ever hoped you'd do something, you'd done it.

But I kind of got over that and was having a good time and drinking this cocktail called Twinkle Toes and asking him some questions about whether he would ever want to live in Paris and stuff like that. And then, maybe like half an hour in, when I had finished my first cocktail and was trying to get the waitress's attention, I zoned into what he was saying because he wouldn't fucking draw breath to let me call the waitress over and he hadn't looked at the menu or anything. And I realised that everything he was saying about the future and the things he wanted to do was totally about himself as an individual. The places he wanted to visit, the jobs he wanted to do, the money he wanted to make. All of it was bullshit, obviously. It was all pub talk. But listening to him, it was as if I didn't exist in his vision of the future at all. I only mattered, at the restaurant on our anniversary trip, or in this imagined future, as an audience to his one-man show. The first date my husband took me on, she said, he said things like, 'When we get married' or, 'When we have kids'. He asked me questions about cities I wanted to visit and how I imagined my life to be.

Did it turn out like that? I asked. Is it how you imagined it?

She smiled.

Not really. But I like that he asked.

How you felt in Paris, I said, was how I felt the entire time I was away.

I thought you would never come back. You never called home. When you did come home, you were like a totally different person. You wouldn't talk about it – you would get angry if we asked you anything.

My twenty-first birthday, I said, looking at her.

She nods.

It was awful. Watching you cry at dinner when Mum and I came up for the day. You looked haunted, she said.

Yeah, I said. I had no idea who I was. I felt like I was just – I picked up the baby and put her on my knee – absorbed into him. I felt like I was looking for myself everywhere, I said. Does that make sense?

Kind of, she said. I remember that it took you ages to make any decision. Like you didn't know what you liked any more.

~

I am almost exactly how I imagined I would grow up to be. Almost. I didn't become a famous actress, I didn't even try, and I sweep a lot more than I thought I would, but that's a waitress thing. Other than that, I know that I am the woman I dreamt of becoming. I especially feel this way when I am by myself. When I make coffee just for me and I know how to do it and I don't burn myself. The novelty of it. A fridge with cheese that I have bought because I like it. Daffodils on the windowsill in a vase I bought with my pocket money when I was eight. The vase has a cow on it and I wipe dust off its nose while I wait for the steam to start. Old, good music that my father used to play in the truck. Ella and Louis and Crystal Gayle, who, when I first heard her, made me feel like I was sitting in a jazz bar surrounded by smoke, even though I was six and had never been in one, just seen pictures. I drink my coffee and I eat my cheese and I dance around the jewel box apartment in an old denim shirt and I remember what it was like to want these things. To want to be grown up.

My vision of myself as a grown-up has come true so completely that I think I must have known it would happen. I must have been able to see myself in the future in order to follow the thread so perfectly. I used to imagine myself, tall and beautiful, in a room full of books. I saw myself going up on tippy toes in someone's forgotten shirt to get a book down from a high shelf. Light from an unknown window hitting the soles of my feet.

I have another one, another image of myself in the future. I've had it for years. It feels like a memory of something that is yet to happen and so it's not slippery, the way daydreams are. There is a long, low stone cottage. The stones are warm and yellow, and there are red geraniums growing in a thin bed that runs along the front of the house. It is hot. I walk up to the cottage and knock on the door. Grasshoppers talk about me. Warmth bounces off the stones and when I begin to get impatient and suspect nobody is home, the big wooden door swings open and there I am. I stand there, with the baby on my hip. I am wearing a white camisole and a long red skirt and there is flour all over me and the baby, as if I've just stopped baking. The version of me holding the baby says,

What?

And in that moment I know that I live there by myself and that any other option is an impossibility.

Sometimes my mother says,
    You two are the best things that ever happened to me.
    And sometimes she says,
    I never should have had children.

The first time I met you, at that dinner where I wore that dress that made you actually swallow like a cartoon character, we spoke about children. We sat next to each other. When someone made a joke we looked at each other so we could laugh together and I wondered how far I would have to stretch my toes before they bumped into your shin. You said,
    Do you want to have kids?
    Sure, I said. But I don't want to look after them. I smiled my cat-who-wants-the-cream smile.
    You laughed.
    Well, I've always wanted to be a stay-at-home dad.
    She'll be a lucky woman, I said.

When my sister leaves, she pauses in the hallway. The baby on her hip. Their cheeks the same shade of wild-rose pink in the glow coming through the skylight.
    She says,
    You are allowed to be happy, you know. It's OK to want to be loved.
    I know, I said. It's just not the only thing that I want.

~

In a land not so far from this one, back when men could have what they wanted just by wishing, a woman found herself blessed with a child. This was surprising, as the woman had done everything in her power to prevent such a blessing.

Her husband had been chosen by her father, or rather, the husband had bribed her father and the woman married this man who made her skin crawl like a snake on its way to an apple tree. In truth, the father was happy to see her go. She was disobedient. She wore heeled shoes and read too much.

You will not find her a good wife, the father said. Take my other daughter. She was cursed by an evil witch and cannot speak, but you will find her pure and beautiful and good.

No, the future husband said. This one will learn.

The woman found herself pregnant despite her frequent trips to the evil witch who lived at the crossroads and despite the scratch marks that crisscross the man's neck.

The child died during the birth. The husband found the wife kneeling, clutching the red bundle, and knew she had killed the child. Accidents don't happen in stories like these. He thought of the witch. He thought of the way his wife writhed when he touched her. Like a slug in salt.

Oh, also, the husband is the king. Everyone loves him. So, when he decides to put the wife to death, because she seduced him, disobeyed him, and murdered his son, everyone goes with it. She is killed by being thrown into a vat of oil full of poisonous snakes. They make the witch watch and then they kill her too.

The king marries the other sister, the one who can't speak. The marriage is a success. They have many children. Peace is restored in the kingdom.

Day Four

or

Abounding in Songs and Legends

I didn't know what to do with myself the day after my sister visited. It was my first day off since you'd left and I checked my phone so often that eventually I threw it across the room, wincing when it skittered to a halt against the skirting board even though I threw it with the intention of hurting it.

My mother called. In the background, I could hear pots bubbling on the stove. The click of the spatula against the metal. Although she had called me, she started the conversation with,

Hang on, darling. I'm cooking.

Last time I visited her, she had a stack of books next to her bed. A third edition of *How to Overcome Depression*. A field guide to the Camino de Santiago. A DK *Encyclopedia of England's Kings and Queens* and a magazine that I had a story published in. Lined up neatly with the spines aligned.

Are you all right? she asked.

Yeah, I'm fine.

Why don't you just come home? she said.

I have to work, I said.

I didn't tell her that every time I came back to our apartment I imagined you here, all the way up the road, right until I opened the front door. I convinced myself you'd be there and I walked faster. I looked in every room.

Did he say when he was coming back?

Yeah, I said. At the end of the week.

Well, she said – and I know she is holding herself back from saying more, a hard-learnt lesson from years in which I never listened to anything she said – just remember, you are going to live a charmed life. And I love you.

Mum?

Yes, darling?

Is being married just the worst?

She laughed.

No, it's not. But it's hard work. You know what I always say.

We say it together.

I shouldn't have married anyone.

It's different these days, she said. You girls have so much more choice than I did.

It doesn't feel that different, I said.

What went wrong? she asked.

I don't tell her the truth, which sounds insane. I made

it wrong. I lost you in my mind long before you packed your bags.

Have you heard from him?

No, I said. Not since he left.

You used to text me things like,

This is rubbish. What did I do before you?

when I went away.

~

When we graduated, nobody wanted to move. We loved it here too much. All our friends, the friendly north wind, the purple nights of summer. So we didn't. You got a job at a restaurant by the harbour, working long hours. You came to my house with new scars every day from shucking oysters. On your first day, an eel wrapped itself up your arm, right up to the shoulder, like a sea monster. I stayed at my restaurant. Wrote in quiet moments behind the bar. I would pick you up from your place on the way home. The back entrance of the kitchen a rectangle of light in the dark alleyway. The click of my shoes on the sidewalk. Your boss came to the door once instead of you. He looks like you. The same dark curls. Grey in his. Moving slow like a big cat. He leant in the doorway for a second. Bleach and smoke.

He's on his way. You want a drink or something?

I said no and you came out a couple of minutes later, laughing.

What did he say? I asked.

What everyone always says.

Tell me anyway, I said, slipping my hand into the back pocket of your jeans. The night empty except for the lonely gulls flying quietly in the black, and us.

No, you laughed, it'll go to your head. Pushing your bike with one hand and holding me with the other.

You cycled in a way that terrified me. No helmet, sometimes drunk out of your mind.

Hey, I said, watching you wrestle your bike out from behind my clothes rail, buy a fucking helmet.

I'm a good cyclist, you said.

Yeah, well, if you die you're going to ruin my life.

I had so many nightmares as a kid about my parents dying. I used to stay up late to watch my mum drive home from work. I used to wait, my face pressed against the glass of my bedroom window, for her headlights to swoop up the road. Sometimes, I even cried with relief. That feeling of barely escaping. When my mother sat me and my sister on the edge of a bed in a hotel near the hospital and told us my dad was dying, I wasn't surprised. I thought I had made it happen by fearing it so much. My mother says worrying is a prayer for disaster.

Two Shot always tells me that the world, thank God, does not revolve around me.

You don't have the power to make bad things happen, she said to me one morning in a worn-out November. I was sitting on the breakfast bar, my legs tucked up into my sweater like a small child. I'd been trying not to cry.

But I think all these bad things are going to happen, and then they kind of do, because when I'm worried I act weird and I get all . . . I flailed my arms in the air. It meant chaotic, intense.

Listen to me, she said. You are smart. You are intuitive. But you cannot control the events of the world with your thoughts. I promise you.

Yeah, I guess.

Do you have weirdly prophetic dreams? she asked.

She flipped the eggs in the pan for emphasis.

Yes you do. Can you boil an egg perfectly soft each time without setting a timer? She looked at me, her eyebrows raised.

Can you? she repeated.

Yes, I said, in a small voice.

Do animals and birds really like you?

I laughed.

Yes they do, she continued, and honestly it pisses me off. You're like a fucking Disney princess. But are you responsible for the bad behaviour of men you're sleeping with, just because you get anxious and want some fucking reassurance from these sons of bitches?

The kettle went off with a click and she set her spatula down and poured boiling water into our mugs. Hers had Poldark on it. My mum had bought it for her.

But sometimes I feel like I know that bad things are going to happen, I said. Sometimes I feel like I'm cursed.

She put down my cup of tea and placed her hand on the cold foot poking out from the bottom of my sweater.

You are not a bad person. You do not attract bad things. I do think that you know a lot of stuff. I do think that, at the very least, you are a witch of boiled eggs. Which, don't get me wrong, would be enough to burn you at the stake. But you aren't running this whole show, baby.

My mother says she can count the marriages she admires on one hand. Now I say the same thing, but normally I say 'relationships' because none of our friends are married yet. At some point, my mother says, it changes. You marry someone and you love them and then you wake up one day and you can't stand them any more.

When does it happen? I asked her. After five years or ten, or after you have kids?

It just happens, she said. All the things that brought you

together in the first place burn away. And you have to make do with what you have left.

Then why would anyone do it? I asked.

She sighed down the phone.

People think it won't happen to them.

Everyone thought we were crazy when we moved into our cramped apartment together. We'd only been dating for a year. The first of our friends to fall.

How is it? they would ask us in hushed tones.

How's it going?

Like an aunt, hunting for misery at a family party.

~

You asked me to move in with you on our trip to visit your mother, that first time you took me to Denmark. All my memories of being there flicker at the edges and make my eyes sting. The fire in your mother's house, the way you laid down a blanket and kissed me in front of it. I had splinters in my hair. You sang 'Smoke Gets in Your Eyes' and made me laugh. The frogs in the garage, tens of them, tiny and wet and hopping high like hard rain splashing against pavement.

The land there is flat and only starts to roll over itself when it gets closer to the sea. Grass hangs on to the sand dunes by its fingernails and screams when the wind from the west rips through it.

There are wolves in the woods, your mother's husband told me. They've been brought here, from Germany.

What a life it must be to lack risk so profoundly that you import it from foreign countries. I felt it even then, that pull in the pit of my stomach. That old desire to chew my own foot off.

Remember those old dresses I got from that house called Isold? People name their houses there, as if they have long, knobbly legs curled up under the foundations and might spring up and away at any moment. The farmhouse loomed over me. There were songbirds perched all along the spine of her thatched roof. They had their faces pointed to the sun but every now and then one of them looked down at me and giggled to her neighbour about my dirty-kneed jeans and the scarf that held my hair back. Clumps of grass rose out of the thatch in optimistic groups, springing like hair from the face of a fine-boned old woman.

Hero,
    you called from inside the garage.
    Hero, are you coming?
The garage was dark and filled with piles of things that teetered and were held together by beams of light and abandoned cobwebs. A soup boat balanced atop a stack of magazines from 1968. There was a doll's house with cutlery

in it, dotted throughout the rooms. Tiny women contending with monstrous knives in their hallways.

When my dad died, we sold loads of stuff to strangers in a garage like this, I said.

Like a car boot sale? you said, holding up a green wine glass so that it caught the light.

Yeah, we called it a garage sale, though.

Inventive, you said.

I smiled, and ran my hand along your back as I walked by.

Is anyone home? I asked.

There was a sign pinned to the wooden door that led into the house. The door was the colour of caramel. I suspected the whole house was made of candy.

No one's home.

Look at these dresses, I said.

A row of them hanging there.

Yeah, my mum said there would be clothes here. They're all her friend's, you said.

Why is she getting rid of them?

I think they're from when she was younger and used to travel a lot for work and stuff. She was a neuroscientist before she got married.

You pushed a pram back and forth absent-mindedly while you spoke.

What does her husband do? I asked.

Oh, he left her. Years ago.

Oh.

Yeah. For her daughter's best friend.

Oh my God.

Yeah, she bought this house with the money from the divorce, and now she runs this little second-hand thing and sells honey from the garden.

Does she live with anyone?

No, she's here by herself I think, you said. You held up a fondue set questioningly. I shook my head.

Can we buy some honey? I asked.

Sure, you said.

Do you think it's OK if I try these on?

My dirty feet hidden by the hem of the dress. The material rustling like bright green leaves in a July breeze. I walked barefoot into the garage. The woman, who had just come home, spun on her heel and looked at me and, in that light, her silver hair could've been gold. She smiled. She said something to you.

She's giving it to you, you said.

You paused to listen to the golden-haired woman.

She said it looks like yours already.

Your mother took us to visit a shepherdess.

She's amazing, she said over her shoulder, eyes on the curving road running through the flat country, she's lived out here for years. Sometimes we get meat from her and it's delicious. So rich and tender.

The sheepskin we bought from her is crushed now. It's draped on my writing chair. For a while, it smelt like lanolin. It made my fingers oily. But all of that has worn off. It makes it feel dead; it reminds me that something had to be killed for me to have it.

We are having such trouble with the wolves here, the shepherdess said.

She spoke in English for me. The women there remember that I am at the table too. You were outside, touring the barns with some of the men.

The wolves? I said. The ones that they brought from Germany?

No, no, these ones, they came across the border on their own. They are looking for . . . for . . . more food, and new places to live.

Have they eaten any sheep? I asked.

Other men stood in the kitchen, cutting slices of cheese and chattering, leaving muddy marks on the stone floor. Rain tapped gently at the window. The lady next to me was spinning raw wool into yarn. The click of the loom made me sleepy, the afternoon had shuddered into night. Candlelight pooled across the room.

Yes, but it's not so bad that they eat one sheep, or two sheep. These wolves, they're bad wolves.

These ones are very bad, the woman sitting beside me added. The skin around her eyes had set into a permanent smile. I smiled looking at her.

Bad in what way?

The shepherdess leant forward, tapping the table top with her fingertips as she spoke.

They do not come and eat a sheep one day and then in a week come back and take another sheep. No, they come and they seem to almost . . . she paused, waved her hands in the air in distress . . . take a bite out of every sheep they can. They bite one sheep – she slammed her fist on the table top – they do not finish this sheep, they keep going and they – she slammed the table again – bite and bite until many sheep are injured and the rest are—

She finished the sentence in Danish.

Scared? I offered.

Scared, she said. This shepherdess had her hair held up by a piece of red felted wool. She drank almost an entire jug of coffee by herself and said 'shit' so many times since I'd arrived in the kitchen that I was tempted to say it to keep her company.

Shit, I said. She smiled.

The old women wear their hair long there. From the back, they look like girls, walking through the farmyard in their mothers' sweaters. The woman knitting beside me, her hair had golden strands ribboned through the grey, the same shade as mine. I wanted to put my head on her shoulder.

And now, the shepherdess said, the dog that I bought for the sheep, he is so scared that he cannot do anything.

The guardian dog?

Yes, I think he, because there were maybe many wolves, not only one, he is scared also and he does not want to go back into the field.

So what will you do? I asked her. There was a carved shepherdess crook with a gold top leaning in the corner of the room. The men tramped back out to work and the room was quiet, save for the clicking of needles and the thrum of rain against the window. My hair was damp and I pulled the cuffs of your old Norwegian sweater over my hands. I had dirt under my nails.

Every night until I move the sheep away from this place, I will go and sit with a fire, to watch, she says.

The wolves – the woman next to me added – they hate the fire. They see it and they know that these sheep they . . . she paused.

They're protected, I said. She nodded.

So you're going to go tonight and sleep out there? I asked, looking out the window at the rain.

I won't sleep, the shepherdess said. I blushed.

What about the dog? I said.

He is in the yard, the shepherdess said, gesturing with disdain out of one of the low windows.

I stood up and peered out. There was a large white dog, asleep, pressed up close to the stable door. A chicken lay curled on its soft, fat belly. A man walked past with a bucket and stopped for a moment to pet the dog, who thumped his tail with gratitude.

Next time you come, I will show you how to make this, the golden-haired lady said from behind me. I turned, and she held up a brown woollen sweater, with a large hood.

It's raw wool, she said. If you walk in this, you will not be touched by the rain.

We drove for an hour to meet the shepherdess in the spot where she spent the night, not sleeping. The field where we found her was hissing. It gave off the kettle-like steam of the early morning. Swallows were darting close to the ground and skimming over the sheep before roaring back into the sky. It made me dizzy to watch them. Your mother and your stepfather had backpacks on, which bulged with the outline of sensible things. Coffee flasks. Sandwiches wrapped in tinfoil, with initials on them. Apples from the orchard that were so tart that I grimaced when I ate them in hesitant bites.

Here we are, your mother said to the shepherdess, who was standing at the edge of the flock, her weight resting on one leg. Her fingers played absent-mindedly in the wool of a sheep.

We're going to go this way, she said. With her crook she pointed to the disappearing rise of the hill ahead of us.

One of the sheepdogs didn't want to do any work. She

trotted behind me in the heather with her bubble-gum tongue lolling out and head-butted the back of my legs whenever I stopped walking. I walked a little apart from the group. I turned the angle of my face so that all I could see was the sheep and the dogs and the land rolling out from the spot under my feet. The shepherdess came up next to me.

This one wants to play, I said, laughing at the dog's face against my leg.

Yes, she needs instruction. The shepherdess smiled down at the dog indulgently.

But if you tell her to do something, is she good?

The shepherdess whistled and the dog took off across the ground so fast that turf flew out behind her. It looked weightless for a moment before it rained back down in thudding clods.

Why do the swallows fly so low? I asked.

You and your family were catching up.

They are trying to eat the bugs that come with the sheep.

They're beautiful.

Yes. I like them a lot, the shepherdess said.

I moved away before you reached me. I took a dog with me.

The shepherdess told me she found a sheep that had broken both of its front legs. She could hear it screaming and she found it in a ditch, tangled in a barbed-wire fence. It was when she was new and she didn't have a knife so she bashed its head in with a rock while the other sheep stood there and watched in horrified, blank-eyed silence. You have to love the animals enough to kill them, she told me. You have to be strong enough to kill them when you need to.

Your mother talked about the fish we had in the freezer. Your family had a debate over which film we should watch that evening. The shepherdess was asked good and polite questions.

How far do you walk every day? I asked.

I walk for about four or five hours a day.

By yourself?

Yes, unless we have tourists, she said. I had a slick rain jacket on. I hated it. She had a felted sheepskin tied to her backpack and a knife hanging from her belt.

What made you want to do it?

She looked at the sky.

My husband died.

The dogs lay on the ground in front of us. I threw the stick for them and they sprinted away.

I'm sorry, I said.

And then I lost my farm. The bank, they wouldn't lend me any more money. So. She shrugged.

How did you learn about this?

There was another woman here who was doing it. She let me live on her farm and she bought me these dogs.

And did you love it straight away?

She nodded. The sun had pattered playfully across her face and left footprints on her nose and cheeks. The lines near her eyes flowed outwards over her skin. A river system leading calmly towards the sea.

I love it. The first day I went out by myself – she gestured at the heath – it worked for me.

I envy you, I said.

She looked over her shoulder at my people who tramp towards us through her flowered kingdom. Closing the distance.

It is easy for me, she said. I like to be alone.

~

Before my father died, the longest my mum had been single since she was eighteen was two weeks. She always left someone for someone else. When people ask her what the best days of her life were, she is honest enough to tell them that they were the first couple of years of her widowhood. She hadn't yet met the next man who would break her down into something palatable. She hadn't spent nights waiting for him to call. I used to hear her pacing in the room above mine, and when he finally showed up, I would hear them laughing. Her laughter sounded sharper and more brittle than normal, like it would shatter if hit against something hard.

I think – she says to me – in those first couple of years after your dad died, it was the first time I had ever been

allowed to structure my time how I liked. I had the oppor-
tunity to be the kind of person I wanted to be.

She fell in love with the next man the way you fall into a
cold river on a hot day. Gasping.

We'd never talked about it until she called me while I was
in Denmark. I could hear her crying before I said,
   Hello?
   He doesn't want to do this any more, she said.
   I was sitting by the fire outside your mother's house,
wrapped in a sheepskin with a beer balanced on my knee.
I could hear a fox in the woods behind me, pacing in
the dry leaves. Its small feet keeping time with my wild
heart.
   I called him, she said, and told him I needed some more
commitment. That I needed to feel important to him.
   I could hear her breathing heavily down the phone. When
she cries, her whole face collapses. A cottage falling down
at the first touch of a bulldozer.
   What did he say? I asked.
   He said he couldn't promise me anything more, that he
was giving as much as he could give. I don't understand
what I did wrong.
   Mum, listen to me.
   The owl in the fir tree that towers over the corner of the
house paused to listen as well.

He doesn't care about you. He doesn't give a fuck about you.

I know, she said. I know.

There is no way that you can make this work, I said. It isn't your fault. He wants you to be somebody you're not.

Who? the owl asked.

Men used to throw themselves at my mother's feet. I saw it happen twice in real life. The first time was in the library where she worked. He knelt in front of her and tied her shoelace for her. He looked at her face the whole time. The second time was at a farmers' market and it made me so mad. I wanted her to come look at something I wanted her to buy for me and when I eventually found her she was standing in the thoroughfare, her head back, laughing. A bag full of flowers over her shoulder. A man on his knees in the dust in front of her. When my father first met her he turned his life upside down to get a better glimpse of her. She must be surprised to find herself out of that topsy-turvy world. She must be surprised to be craning to be seen.

The night that you asked me to move in with you, it slipped itself into conversation the way that important things often do. We were out, the two of us; your mother had dropped us at the restaurant like we were teenagers. We watched an older couple arguing at the next table. The ice melting in his cocktail, the glass sweating. Water pooling on the dark-wood table like an oil slick on an ocean. Her, sitting curled up tight in her seat.

When we live together, you said, *it won't ever be like that.*

When? I said.

I mean, you blushed, cleared your throat. *It would be nice, I think. And it makes sense –* you dropped your voice, a boy playing at being grown up – *financially.*

Can I have an office?

I think an office is probably outside of our budget, you said.

Can I have my own desk?

I'll try, you said.

Do you promise, I said, holding my hand out, palm up, watching you put yours into it, that it won't be awful?

I promise.

How do you know? I said.

You smiled.

It's different with us.

I thought about my parents. Your parents. All the things I've watched split open and spill. The relationships my mother admires, numbering in single digits. The way I used to cry alone folding the painter's socks the way he liked it done, miles away from the people who loved me. The way I used to wait for him to come home and him ignoring me when he did. I thought about how you told me you loved me in your sleep. How we often woke up fucking. As automatic as pulling your hand away from a flame. I think if you peeled back my skin and muscles you would find your name, scratched like a teenage declaration of fidelity on to the surface of my bones. I thought about the bench in the park by my apartment. It had a brass memorial plaque that said,

JENNY – I LOVE YOU BABY. I'LL SEE YOU IN THAT LONG GOODNIGHT.

I said,

Let's do it.

~

We argued a lot when we first moved in together. About all the usual things.

Can't we buy a dishwasher? I said. I was using the kitchen countertop as a writing desk. My knees pressed into the tumble dryer. My elbows at risk of pushing a stack of glasses into oblivion.

Well, we could, you said. *But we don't have anywhere to put it.*

And I suppose there's no guarantee that it would solve the problem of me having to remind you to do the dishes. I'd be reminding you to put them in the machine instead.

You barely ever have to remind me!

Ah – I said – but why should I ever have to remind you? Because dishes are my jurisdiction?

Oh my God, you said, *if you're going to go off on a Gloria Steinem routine then I'm going to leave you to it. If you need me to help you, ask me.*

You aren't HELPING me – I shouted – you live here.

I'm sorry I'm forgetful, you said, *but it's not my fault that you're more organised than me.*

I thought of, but did not mention, your room at university, which was so immaculate that I was scared of putting a wine glass down without a coaster. I remember thinking the first time I saw it that you were the tidiest man I'd ever met.

I struggled to find my bearings. I felt that old pull, that desire to blend so totally with somebody else that you forget who you are. I would wake up amazed to find you there. I used to tell people that after I graduated I would buy a boat and live on it with a Border Collie. I'd moor the boat in the harbour of the town where I was born, where the pines run right down to the water and people pick salmonberries on the beach. I dreamt about writing in the cabin next to a small wood-burning stove. In these visions I am listening, almost exclusively, to Joni Mitchell. I am jumping off the boat into the black water. Look. The dog is jumping in too. I am wrapping myself in an old, scratchy towel and reading on the bow. There I am. All by myself.

You asked me once, on a night where we hadn't unpacked all our things and were eating lasagna, sitting on the floor, using a cardboard box as a table,

When do you feel most yourself?

I said,

When I'm writing.

These days, writing is different. I feel a pull towards it the way men feel a pull towards the sea. It lurches like an old truck out of a driveway. I damp it down. I pour myself wine at 4 p.m. and I can't write when I've been drinking so I watch reality TV standing up in the kitchen to smooth my brain out.

The first time we ever had a horrible fight was because you contradicted me about something until I was in tears. You googled what I was saying as I was saying it. When it turned out I was right, you didn't back down, you just said I'd got lucky, that it was pure chance that I knew something that you didn't. After I slammed the door behind me and left you in the hallway, and after I had gone a couple of streets away and calmed down enough to notice that the air smelt like jasmine and that the light was soft and tactile, I couldn't stop shaking my head. Not at you – at myself, for thinking that it would be different.

So stupid, I said aloud.

Black butterflies fluttering around my ankles.

We joked sometimes that you were Hades and I was Persephone, and I wonder which translation we're in. Is it the one where I glance at things to bring them to life? Me, teaching you how to plant daffodils and drink honeysuckle and crush chamomile between your fingers to smell the tart green appleness of it. Or the one where I'm trapped with the dead, a corpse bride myself?

~

On the evening of the fourth day, I invited people to dinner and tidied the apartment half-heartedly, scrunching up clothes and shoving them into drawers. I thought about turning the photo of you to the wall. But that made it seem like you had died and I didn't want to tempt fate. In arguments with the painter, I would experience *déjà vu* so severe that I knew what he was going to say before he said it. I knew the next part of the story.

The Maidens came, along with other girlfriends. One of them talked about getting back together with an ex-boyfriend. She showed the messages he sent. We pointed out the spelling mistakes in them and told her that anyone who calls you an insecure bitch who doesn't know what's good for you and needs to be taught how to behave, doesn't care about you. I said,

People who treat you like this don't love you. It's that simple.

She shook her head.

It's OK, she said.

He can sometimes be so kind to her, so patient. He just wants the best for me, she said (this is a fiction), he wants me to be the most independent version of myself and like, less insecure and stuff (this is a myth). We're going to move in together. Be happy for me, she said.

She had, earlier in the evening, told us that he often forgot to wipe his ass after he went to the toilet. She would routinely be doing the laundry and find crusted streaks of shit in his underwear that she then scrubbed out by hand before putting them on to wash with the rest of the clothes. He did it so often that sometimes when he went to the bathroom, she would ask him if he'd remembered to wipe when he came out. I was already a little drunk when she told us this and said,

How can you fuck someone whose shit you see, unconsensually, on a regular basis?

It's not easy, she said. He is a bit – and she smiled in this indulgent way – like a big baby.

Disgust pooled in my lower back. I was sweating.

I like that he relies on me, she said.

Does he like, I said, focusing my gaze like an archer, do nice stuff for you?

Like what?

I don't know, the classics. Does he ask you about your day and buy you jewellery and make your life better?

He definitely makes my life better.

But how, though? I said. I was leaning forward. The Kid and Tex exchanged a look.

I like having him around, she said, smiling, but her eyes were a little too bright. I like having someone to go to museums with and go out to dinner with. And I want to get married and have kids soon.

Why?

Outside, a fox screeched with rage. Or want – it's hard to tell the difference. The sky was clear and peppered with the impassive glare of faraway stars. In the pause, Tex got up and got another bottle of wine.

You don't need to do that, I said. I can do it.

I want you to relax, she said.

I don't invite you to my house so you can do things, I said. You're supposed to be relaxing.

The wine was red and cold. Thin, like blood.

Why? I asked again.

Because I've always wanted to get married and have babies. It'll make me happy.

Are you happy now? I asked.

What – Two Shot, following me into the kitchen – the fuck is going on in her mind?

God, it's so depressing, I said, leaning my weight against the counter.

Do you think he's changed? she asked me.

I doubt it, I said. But even if he has, how much better can he possibly be? People don't change that much. And why would he? If he can act however he wants and she doesn't leave, why would he change his behaviour?

A car roaring too fast on a night-time street. The feeling of thinking quietly to yourself: somebody is going to get hurt.

I don't get why she puts up with it, I said.

I don't get it, she said, but I know why she does it.

Why?

Because she thinks it's better than being alone.

When the others left, we turned the lights down and put on James Taylor. Two Shot flipped on the lava lamp you bought me for our second anniversary. The room glowed the kind of red that wants to be purple. The walls dappled with bruises. We opened all the windows and lit cigarettes – Karelias. We like the way the pack opens up like a cigar box. Like you're the heroine of a Raymond Chandler movie. The women in his films are so deranged that my friends and I shout,

ICON,

at the screen when they come down to breakfast in a backless sequinned dress or poison a child.

So, The Kid said, how are you?

I'm fine, I said. How are you?

Don't be facetious, she said.

I am fine. I don't want to talk about it. Can't we just have fun?

How long left till he comes back? The Kid asked, frowning.

Three days.

Are you writing about it? Two Shot asked me.

I blew a smoke ring. I have recently learnt how to do it and am willing to kill myself to be able to do it properly. The moon turns her face away.

No, I said.

It rained today. Down on the street, water is pooling in the gaps between the cobblestones. Flowers grow from there, such brave ones. One of my favourite things about the city is how you can hear the river underneath it after it rains. Those hidden creeks say, sure it looks like a city. But underneath it's different. Take up the road and you'll find the river. You cannot kill a forest. You can just make it wait.

Don't you think it might help? The Kid asked.

Yeah, maybe.

Doesn't writing normally make you feel better?

A bit. Sometimes when I write things down, it's like it stops being me. And when I can see all the bits on the page like that, it's easier to see myself as a whole person.

I hate to lower the tone, Two Shot said, but before you love anyone else you have to love yourself. Which is a bit tricky if you've never been allowed to know who you are.

My mother's friend said to me once,

Listen, you might think you love him, but at some point, he's just going to be an old, gross guy sitting on your couch.

I don't think I'll ever feel that way about him, I said.

She laughed.

Everybody thinks that.

~

Zelda Fitzgerald died in a fire at a sanatorium where she was placed for many reasons, one of them being that she had a 'complex' about writing. When I search her name, tap-tap-tapping it out with my fingers, pictures come up of the place where she burnt to death. '10 Eerie Photos of Abandoned Mental Asylum where F. Scott Fitzgerald's Wife Died'. 'How Crazy Was Zelda?' offers a *New York Times* article, written the year I was born. Zelda wanted to be a writer. She told her ideas to Hemingway. She waved her hands around when she spoke, her weight rocking on the red leather couch of some Paris salon. Pernod slopping over the edge of her glass, a little too much of her, a little too enthusiastic. He dismissed her, which is an accusation that we cannot level at her husband. F. Scott used parts of her diaries in his work. They were collaborators, he used her ideas, he cosigned her stories (for marketing reasons, we are told, and I believe that; I know how these flesh markets work). He admitted that their conversations and, sometimes, her writing, fed into his own work. There is no shame in this; art is a process of stealing. It is piratical by nature.

But when she finally wrote a book, finally, after years of labour, after years of trying to carve out space for herself, F. Scott read it and demanded that everything that resembled his work be struck out. He decided that he actually did not want to share ideas. Not his, anyway. What's yours is mine.

And what's mine is mine.

It doesn't surprise me that she burnt to death, tied to a life she had never consented to. Hands bound. Lips blue. Prophecies congealing in her throat. She wanted to be good at something. Fire licking the feet of a woman who had never, not once, been allowed to run.

The writing programme I attend runs a workshop on defamation. They remind us that Knausgård's family don't talk to him any more. I feel like reminding them that when men write about themselves, they are heroes. When Elizabeth Smart does it, people write reviews so hysterically negative that one feels like offering the reviewer a glass of water and a little lie-down.

You said, soon after we moved in together,

I'd rather you didn't write about me. Or about us, you added. I closed my laptop and turned round in my chair.

No one will know that it's you, I said. It's not like I've said he's six feet tall and has brown hair and his dad lives in America.

That's not the point, you said, frowning. *I don't want to feel like everything that happens between us is material for your work.*

Why not?

It makes me feel used.

OK, I said. Then, when you looked at me as if you were expecting something, I added, sorry.

If you're going to write about me, make me seem nice, you said. And then, after a pause,

I am nice, aren't I?

In class, we went around and talked about why we do it.

When I said,

I like the control. I like being the one who writes the story.

Another woman put her hand on her chest.

Oh, honey, she said, true writing always has to come from the heart.

I know that. This is what my heart looks like. It has boot marks on it.

You don't like being looked at and you deserve autonomy. But so do I. And I'm not sure that if we're going head to head on freedom that I should lose on a technicality. It's like when we used to argue about what name the babies would get.

They can have your last name as a middle name, you said.

My dad is fucking dead, I said. Jesus Christ, I want them to have my name as a last name, not as some second-rate middle name they'll never use.

It's too many names, you said. *I have a double-barrelled last name and I hate it.*

OK, amazing, I said. Then they can have mine.

You looked at me like I was insane. That option, it seemed, hadn't occurred to you.

~

If the world wasn't ending and we had more money I'd want loads of kids, you said.

We were leaning over the edge of our balcony watching a mother herd her small daughter and very small daughter up the hill that runs past our apartment. The little one kept saying,

You're going too f-a-a-s-t – dragging the word out while she pumped her toy-sized arms, trying to catch up. She had a baby doll clamped under one armpit. You were smiling at her. I was smiling at you.

My sister, whenever she calls me, is almost impossible to hear because of the baby in the background. I love the baby but I catch myself frowning when she screams over our conversation. When the baby was first born, my mother and I stayed with my sister for a night. The baby would not settle and screamed like a pig stuck in a gate, and we paced anxiously, unable to help. The next morning, my mother said,

God, when babies make noise like that it makes you realise how awful it would be to have one if you didn't want one.

She looked at me and I nodded. My sister constantly asks when I am going to have a baby.

It would be so cute, she says.

I think of my niece, secretly, as my baby, or at least our family's baby. Sprung miraculously from our family of women with no need for a man, divine or otherwise. She recognises me when she sees me and smiles in a slow, creeping way, as if she is understanding a joke. She has learnt to want things and wants to hold my finger when we push her in the pram. I dance for her and she looks at me wide eyed before copying me, flinging her little body from side to side, pausing frequently to make sure I'm watching. My sister, when the baby was six months old, came for a sleepover. You vacated the apartment for the occasion, a six-pack of Bud in your bag to take to your friend's. The baby had a bath and squeaked until I came in to watch her and my sister, naked and splashing under-neath the creeping watchfulness of my Devil's Ivy. When we slept, the three of us together in bed, I barely breathed, terrified of accidentally hurting her. She threw a leg over me, just like I used to do with my dad. I felt grateful for the attention. In the morning she put her whole hand in my mouth to wake me up.

A fox in heat keeps screaming outside the window. I don't know if it's the same one that used to wake you up. I read a story once about a woman who was murdered. A man played a cassette on a boombox outside her house that sounded like a crying baby and she went to check on it and that's how all her body parts ended up isolated from each other. It was the care that killed her.

The first time we slept together, you woke up the next morning and shuffled down the bed. You kissed my stomach. You looked at me and said,

This is my favourite bit.

Years later, you watched me playing with my niece. You smiled in that way that made your eyes crinkle up, in that way that makes you look like a boy. I knew what you were thinking. Am I the only one who can feel it? The way all of this was written for me, the way all my attempts to get myself out drive the ruts deeper. This is a myth. Do you want to be Mary or Medea?

Do you ever feel, Two Shot asked, worried that if your work gets published you'll lose people?

She's lounging in the rocking chair you bought me. She's playing with her penknife, flicking it lazily open then closed with the relaxed superiority of a mountain lion sharpening her claws.

No, I don't worry about that, I said.

Really? I would, she said.

Well, it's a good thing that you're a ceramicist, I said.

But, she said, leaning forwards, the knife catching the light – and I remember reading something about how good murderers paint their knives black so their victims aren't warned by the last light they'll ever see – do you think that if it gets published people will call you and be, like, fuck you?

I laughed.

I think that's likely. But, I already decided, I said.

Faustian, she said.

Exactly. I sold my soul to the devil so I confess about my sins.

Oh, please, The Kid said, you sold your soul to the devil so you could journal.

The other day, I said, a writer from my class asked if I wrote about myself because I didn't have any imag- ination, or because I found myself really interesting. He was waggling his finger at me, like I was some kind of naughty French schoolgirl begging to be spanked.

What a cunt, Two Shot said.

Men hate when women find themselves interesting, The Kid said.

Why do you think that is?

Because then they don't get the pleasure of giving you a sense of self, she said.

~

I am not going to name the men in this story, so don't worry if you can't keep track of which boy I am talking about. It makes no difference. There was a boy. He worked part time at a butcher's that all the chefs I knew loved because they did whole animal butchery; a dying art. Carcasses, dry-ageing in the back room. A regiment of knives clinging to the wall in one long orderly line. He has several chips on his shoulders and the borders of them are sharp. He wears mostly black. He has pointy teeth and reservoir eyes. Man made depth. Cold and unsafe. There is moss on the concrete banks. You lose your footing and no one is there.

The butcher and I, we'd been friends for a while but he would sigh when I walked into the wipe-clean room where he worked. He would whisper,

Fuck,

when I walked through the door in my little black boots and my evergreen miniskirt. He would give me things for free. Frying steaks, wrapped in weeping brown paper like he was Stanley and I was his pretty star. He was built like Marlon but nowhere near as charismatic, and it was no problem at all because I have a good imagination and I filled in the gaps for him. I dreamt him as better than he was and liked him best when I hadn't seen him in a while. I felt disappointed when I did see him – his long hair not as thick or shiny as the rich chestnut I remembered. His high cheekbones still there, but the beard that hung off his jaw less full than it was when I imagined it scratching the soft skin of my pussy. He gave me chunks of fatty belly that I would roast and serve to other men. Jars of animal things preserved in liquid, like the horrors down the road at the medical museum.

You're so cool, he'd say, and I'd laugh and do that thing where I'd wait for him to go to his bench with the saw and then I'd put ChapStick on slowly and catch him watching me and laugh again, as if it was all a silly mistake. I looked at him from under my lashes. I blinked slowly like a kitty cat hoping that when my eyes opened, they would look how they look in my head: pale as ice with vertical pupils.

I met up with him one night at a bar that made me blush whenever I walked into it because I had asked the manager out when I was sloppy drunk and then cancelled my date with him because I started sleeping with someone else, who he was, in fact, friends with. The man I slept with instead, he told me they talked about me.

What do you talk about? I asked, playfully. I tilted my head to one side like a puppy.

Oh, I can't, I don't want to . . . He took off his beanie and ran his hands through his hair. We were sitting in the park. I was doing a good job of pretending to be interested in anything other than how his face looked when I undid his belt with my teeth. Grass starting to get wet with the promise of evening.

What, you can't tell me? I said.

I can't tell you. He looked at his lap.

That good, huh? I said.

The evening I met the butcher in that bar, I drank 12% beer. I drank La Chouffe and other beers that other men had bought me in foreign countries. I ate olives and licked brine drips off my wrist. Who knows what we talked about. I can see myself through the candlelit window, with my tongue in his mouth, sitting on a rickety stool in the corner.

Just so you know, I said, I'm not looking for anything intense.

Sure, he said. Breathing hard.

When I started to unlock the dark green door that led to the cool quiet of my building's stone hallway, he grabbed me by the throat and pushed me up against the wall. Someone walked out of the building and had to brush past us. I was very aware of my tongue. It was the only part of me that was moving. Twitching restlessly in my mouth, looking for an escape route. I swallowed the gasp when he let go of me.

And they didn't say anything? Two Shot asked the next day.

What would they have said? Hey, babe, are you into choking? Or is he bothering you?

I mean, yeah, she said. They could've checked that you were OK.

I was fine, but it was weird. Who does that? At least ask, you know?

Outside? Choking someone outside on their doorstep? Insane behaviour, she said.

We went upstairs and I pushed him down on the bed and we kissed and he paused and said,

I like you.

And I said,

OK.

We kissed some more. He pulled my hair. My mouth tasted like metal.

The next morning he left at 7 a.m. Months later we went for dinner. He sat opposite me and picked at his food. He was smiling in a dangerous way and I asked him questions about what he had been reading and thinking about.

You're super different in a sexual situation, he said.

Yeah?

Yeah, like, you know what you want. It's kind of intimidating.

Interesting commentary from a man who choked me on my front doorstep. Dangerous to assume I don't know what I want everywhere I go. I didn't say anything. I laughed. I shook my long head of queen's hair. He called me trouble and I thought, well, if you insist.

I am willing to fulfil the prophecies of men less wise than me. If you think I am going to ruin your life, please, don't tell me. I am willing to ruin men who think I am ruinous. I am also willing to destroy men who think I am not.

If you don't want the sirens to sink you, don't get on the ship. Don't sit down below singing songs about the slap of wet flesh and the things you stole from our sea. Don't dream about wrapping your hands around throats. Don't expect victory. Don't lean over the rail and guffaw at the shipwrecks. Whatever you do, don't lounge on the deck and proclaim you aren't scared when you see me rolling and rolling with pleasure in the water, hands in my own hair, wet all over, don't say that you are going to haul me up and put something in my mouth to stop that singing and then throw me back down limp as a fish too small to be eaten. This is a warning. I have written it in the language men understand. Remember Odysseus? Remember the sirens around his ship? If you start down this path, it will not end until one of your friends taps your hand as you sit barely alive at a pub that charges too much for a pint, thinking of the way I rode your body like the crest of a wave, and says,

You all right, buddy?

And you'll shake your head to get the sound of me sighing out of your ears. Can't you hear the sirens? Police cars roaring past the room where I fucked a man who loved me so much he wrote me a letter about it. He wrote it all out on a series of postcards. I used to show them to people at dinner parties I hosted. I read them aloud, sitting on other men's laps. One man's wet dream is another man's nightmare. Can't you hear the sirens? They sound like me, whispering,

I like you,

in the shell-like whorl of your ear. The sirens start singing and they will not stop.

He bought me a copy of *On the Road* to take on my summer trip. I was going to Florence, alone, to visit the Uffizi although when I got there I mainly sat in a square with a small, chirruping fountain and read. He brought it to my work, where I was outside, watering the restaurant's window boxes. I had on a green silk blouse and my hair was held up by a pin. Edith Piaf was coming out of the open door and drifting over the heat-soaked pavement. He said,

Please be careful.

I smiled; I said something noncommittal.

He said,

I don't know what I'd do if something happened to you.

I laughed my bell-chime laugh. I never read the book. I'm never going to.

Later, Tex sent me an article. It was called 'TOP 10 BOOKS FUCK BOYS GIVE WOMEN'. The first one was a Bukowski. The second was *On the Road*. I think that boys believe the things men write about women in books. Women play the opposite of starring roles. They play absence. Recesses. They are tunnels, dark and wet and full of danger, and at the end of the tunnel there isn't a woman but a man who suddenly recognises himself from inside the woman and withdraws, sticky and whole.

The boy said to me,

You're so beautiful I never thought of you as a real person.

And I said,

Really?

But what I thought was, why the fuck have you been friends with me for years if you don't think I'm a real person?

This is a fiction. I am a myth. What is a woman but the product of other people's imaginations?

And of course, he answered my question the night he pushed me up against my front door.

This is why, his hands said.

He found out I was fucking someone else at a wine tasting in the city. Everyone I knew who worked in food ended up there and we were all drunk by 3 p.m. I tried thirty-five champagnes in roughly that many minutes and ate tentacles lightly seasoned with paprika that stained my fingertips orange. I wore a white linen blouse that was transparent in full sunlight. It had been strange between the butcher and me for months because I didn't want to spend time with him. He wanted me too much and I had found out that it wasn't me he wanted but a version of me who would lie there and moan while he did what he thought girls like me wanted. And so when he texted me at three in the morning and said,

I need to see you! I can't stop thinking about you! X

I replied,

I'd love that! x

And then when I saw him lying in the sun on a rare hot day, I would try to move in a way that meant he didn't notice me. I could hear him panting from a great distance. I could feel it on my neck.

At the wine tasting, I sat and chatted with him at first. There is a picture of it somewhere. He is smiling, big. I am looking past the camera to where Two Shot is standing, feet away. I am looking for the exit. Later, I kissed the man I was sleeping with and when I pulled away I saw the butcher stop talking midway through a sentence. Looking at me over the shoulder of someone else on the other side of the room. The words got crushed at the bottom of his throat. And I remember thinking, good. If my body is going to speak over him, it'd better work. He walked out then and there and left all his friends behind, and I laughed and threw my head back and went to get another drink with everyone's eyes following me and I was glad that it made them dislike me. I wanted them to be scared. This is a warning.

Ten minutes after he left he called me. I rolled my eyes and answered.

Two Shot mouthing, Who is it? And when I mouthed his name, she said,

Oh, fuck OFF.

I was laughing when I said,

Hey, what's up?

Yeah, can you meet me outside?

Sure, I said, and I thought: if we are going to have a fight at least it's going to be interesting, but if he wants to cry about it I will laugh and laugh and tell him that I knew what I wanted and what I wanted wasn't him.

He was sitting at the bus stop when I came outside, waiting for something that would never arrive. His hands in his pockets.

Yeah? I said.

Are you fucking kidding me? he said. He stood up. I did not step back.

What are you talking about?

Are you sleeping with him? He gestured inside.

Yeah, I am.

And you didn't think you should tell me?

Why the fuck would I tell you? I laughed. You have a girlfriend. We never dated. Why on earth would I feel like I had to tell you?

We broke up, actually. He threw that information across the few paving slabs separating us like it was going to hurt when it hit me.

So?

So, I broke up with her for you.

I have nothing to say to that.

You know I'm in love with you, he said.

And because you're in love with me, I have to go out with you? I was tapping my foot in my beat-up white sneakers. Another man had eased my foot out of them the summer before and said, we have to get you some new shoes. He had kissed the salty instep of my paw.

No, but—

You've never told me you're in love with me.

You knew, he spat.

I shrugged. I reached into my pocket and put honey-flavoured lip balm on while he quaked opposite me.

It made me feel sick, seeing you two together.

He was crying now. And I was cold, standing outside in the May evening. When I went to walk away, he said,

No,

and circled my wrist with his fingers, not grabbing hard exactly, but resting like a cuff. I turned, imagining, I think, that he would let go, thinking that we were still operating within some realm of normalcy, but he said,

I want to talk to you,

and pulled so that I was knocked off balance and almost fell. He repeated it:

I want to talk to you.

I said,

Let go,

not wrenching my arm out because it would hurt, and he said no and kept talking, his eyes wet with tears and mine rolling like a cow's, the awareness that he wasn't stopping until he was done and he didn't care at all what I wanted making me look from door to door of the houses on the street as if I was expecting one of them to open inwards by magic. My father said that if someone has hold of you and doesn't let go you shouldn't try to fight because you won't win. They will almost always be stronger than you. Don't try to wrestle them off because it wastes time and energy and you shouldn't bother screaming anything, not even 'Fire!' because nobody cares: the people in the park walking by, their eyes down; his friends round the corner, stooped and smoking in the doorway under the nicotine yellow of the streetlight. You have to find a soft place that they won't have thought of protecting

One cheek: scratched in Third Grade in a game of kiss chase, and me in detention for a month

One ear lobe: pinched and twisted like a naughty Dickensian schoolboy to get under the pale, doughy arm and away from the wall at a club, him howling with embarrassment because, I imagine, it made him feel like Oliver Twist

One back of the hand: punctured and bleeding, my favourite hoop earring ruined from stabbing the sharp end of it into the skin

One pinky finger: pulled backwards and broken by my sister in college when a boy pinned her down and wouldn't stop, not even when she said, if you don't fuck off I am going to break your pinky finger

One eye, now: my beer can hitting the sidewalk and hissing with delight, the foam frothing at my feet like I'm being born from the ocean, my fingers plunging into the soft hollow and the feeling of his grip, loosening.

Weeks later I saw him and his girlfriend walking together, holding hands. He had an eye patch. He looked ridiculous. And I felt sorry for her. I heard that he wouldn't tell anyone how it happened. He mumbled when they asked him. When people mentioned it in passing, I said, it was me. I did it. And if he came near me, I'd do it again, but this time, I'd do it harder. This time, I'd blind him.

~

I feel, my mum said, that all the men I've been with wanted me to be something different. Your father, she said, wanted me to love being a wife. I loved him. But there were things about marriage that I just hated. Men, she said, fall in love with women like us because we're vivacious and fun and flirtatious. And then as soon as they have you, they want to pick and choose the parts of you they keep.

Husbands scheduling lobotomies for their wives, paying for the troublesome part of the brain to be scooped out. You don't need that bit, sweetie. The knife cutting through it like a scalpel through an avocado.

I've never, she said, found a way around that. I've seen you do it too, she said.
  Do what?
  Go along with it.

~

164

The story is simple. A widow had two daughters. One was good and one was not. The one who was good and did her chores married a prince who had, up until recently, been a troll. She met the troll while out searching for berries to sustain herself, her mother and her sister ('I am too weak and hobbled by grief,' the widow says), and gave him her food and swept his latrine without protest, out of the goodness of her sweet little heart, and the troll turned into a prince and carried her off to his kingdom. The prince – you guessed it, children, well done – had been cursed by an ugly and wicked witch.

The horrible daughter, who shirks her chores and has no particular desire to sing while she works, sets off into the woods to find another prince troll, at the behest of her emaciated-by-grief and utterly useless mother. But, when the troll asks her to give him her food, she declines, wary of this bog creature who has sprung up from the dark pit of the river to stand in her way. When he asks her to sweep his house, she says,

'No, why should I?'

The troll turns into another prince – there is no word on what made the wicked witch curse the two princes; one assumes it was pure malice – and condemns the second daughter to a lifetime of servitude in her sister's new castle.

As far as I know, she's still there.

Day Five

or

I'm hard to get, Steve. All you have to do is ask me.

I let myself notice that we were nearing the end of a week that I had imagined was permanently fixed, like Christmas decorations on a neglected house, when the phone at the restaurant starts to ring constantly for people wanting to book tables for two on a Friday night. Sometimes, in the middle of the night, I stare at your name on my call history. I try to remember what our last phone call was about. It must have been so small. Do we have milk, how was your day, my mum says hi, I love you. Easily crushed.

Weekend mornings with nothing to do, reading the news in bed and arguing about whether or not Picasso was an asshole. Dancing around the living room to Phil Collins. I always made breakfast. Up first with the radio alarm, making you hot black coffee in the cold months and sweet, iced ones in the summer. Bringing you eggs in bed, you

laughing, saying you lived like a king. You, making dinner
if you were home or leaving it on a plate in the fridge for
me, like a housewife out for a rare evening of freedom.
Monday nights at the movies, cracking beers over the
opening credits that we bought at the off-licence round
the corner. The way we would look at each other when
anything romantic happened on screen. The way we would
look at each other when we saw babies. I loved leaving
things with you. Seeing you across the bar and gesturing
at the door with my head and you nodding and us ricocheting out and saying,

Thank God; I'm so tired,

or,

We're so old now, I can't wait to go home.

My head on your shoulder on the bus. Me dragging my
nails through your hair to help you fall asleep.

I used to say,

I love our life.

And I did. We made it up together. We invented it all by
ourselves.

When we had lived together for a while, I started to get this
itch. My mother says that if the palm of your hand itches,
you are due to come into money. I called her. I said,

Mum, the soles of my feet are itchy all the time. What
does that mean?

It means, she said, you are about to go on a long journey.

Do you ever want to fuck other people? I asked you.

The guy sitting next to me choked on a piece of smacked cucumber. We were at that noodle place we love, the couple next to us were on a first date, he had just asked her what she did and where she lived and what her hobbies were, but they seemed to have run out of conversation and now were sitting in silence while she tried to eat biang biang noodles with one hand and scroll with the other.

Yeah, sometimes. Sometimes, you said, *I see women and think about what it would be like to sleep with them. There was this punky girl on the train today who was* – you laughed – *super hot.*

And super different from me, I guess.

Yeah, you said. *But in real life it isn't like that. You don't go up to beautiful women on the train and get to have sex with them. It's different for women,* you said. *You probably could sleep with anyone you wanted to.*

Do you think about it? you asked me. You leant over and used your napkin to wipe a spot of red oil off my chin.

Yeah, I said, sometimes.

~

When the painter and I had been gone for a while, one of the guys I slept with in school was backpacking around the world and passed through a city at the same time as me. I met up with him. He was getting better looking, losing the blurred softness of adolescence and gaining stubble, which ran a little way down his neck. He had an earring now. It was easier between us than it had been in school, easier than since before we'd fucked on a night where my mum left town and I had a free house. I was reminded why I'd liked him and why I'd stared at him for all those months in photography class. We went to this bar that only sold home-made rum, which they served with bowls of sliced lime. They put the bottle down on the table between us with two small glasses. Our knees touching. The stools low to the ground, the motorbikes hissing by. We talked about writing, art school, our friends back home. I didn't talk about my boyfriend at all. Twinkle lights strung in big, graceful loops through a mimosa tree, the roots of it rippling under the concrete. My boyfriend didn't text me and every time I flipped my phone over and saw nothing I felt the beat of the drum.

I went back to his hostel. The room, which had six sets of bunk beds in it, was amazingly empty. His stomach felt tighter than my boyfriend's. There was something slightly springier about him. When I left, I didn't even rinse my mouth out. I didn't even wash the cum off my hands. I felt, as I walked out on to the road and hailed a taxi, him tracing his fingers up and down my back while I talked, told him some story. I was happier than I had been in months. I felt powerful again, like I was someone. I had recently been feeling see-through.

Lying in bed, we played pioneers. He said,

You're so different from how you used to be. Who are you?

And I said,

Baby, you tell me.

~

You and I went to the National Gallery on one of our rare Saturdays off. It was crowded with children and mums. You waved at the babies as they went past in their prams.

I walked one or two steps behind you. I looked at the back of your neck. You needed a haircut, your hair curled over the collar of your blue silk shirt. In the gallery, there is a picture of Helen of Troy, standing at the edge of a ruined wall. The picture is almost unbearably lonely. She doesn't have a face. I looked at it for a long time. That night, we talked about her.

It is said that Helen was stolen by Theseus because he wanted to marry the daughter of a god. Even at seven, she was too beautiful to resist.

Seven? Helen of Troy was seven when she got kidnapped?

Yeah, I said. But not the kidnapping everyone thinks about – the one with Paris. The first time, by Theseus.

That can't be right.

I told you about the divine wife idea, the right to rule, about Pirithous making the mistake of going for Persephone.

Oh, you said, *so it was more like an 'I'll steal you now and marry you in ten years' kind of deal.*

Well, I said, in some versions, she comes back pregnant.

But if she has a kid then she has to be of childbearing age. She can't be seven or ten, she's got to be at least fourteen.

Not necessarily. Didn't you read about that ten-year-old in America who got denied an abortion? And, I added, the accounts often emphasise her youth and her beauty. Which is insane.

There was a pause. We listened to the swifts who had recently moved into the eaves, screaming like stunt planes before they pull up from the ground.

There must be a version, you said, *where she isn't a child, and she's a teenager.*

OK, I said. Fine.

Helen was sixteen when she was kidnapped by Theseus. She was abducted from her family, raped, impregnated, and then rescued by her brothers. Later, she is abducted again and starts a war with her face. She is despised by her own people, and feared by the people of Troy.

Better? I said.

I think you're looking for the bad in the story, you said.

The first time I took my shirt off in front of you, you said, *I knew your tits would be great. You've got pornstar boobs.*

How did you know?

You laughed.

I've been looking, you said. *You just haven't caught me.*

We had a conversation, right after we first kissed, sitting in the secret booth in that old bar. It has one wall covered with stained-glass windows and the other covered in mirrors, like being inside a dragonfly wing.

I said to you,

Have you only been friends with me for so long because there's always been a chance that you might get to fuck me?

And you agreed.

You took it back. But I haven't forgotten the feeling of living in a world where that's how you felt about me. Maybe the Helen in the gallery is relieved to not have a face. Finally, she thinks, some peace and quiet.

I always feel that Helen of Troy is such an anti-hero, a man said once in a university tutorial. Like, she's so self-satisfied and vain. She reminds me of Patrick Bateman in *American Psycho.*

He drops a chainsaw on a woman, I said.

~

I get stuck on the phrase, make yourself up.

I'm going to make myself up, my mother says, before we leave for a family party.

Girls, listen to me, you have to make yourself up before somebody else does. This is fiction. You're a myth. Pick a good one. I've been Eris recently – it suits me. I've always been deliciously bad, right down to the bone.

Oh, darling, my mother said when I Facetimed her this week, put some lipstick on or something. I know you're having a hard time, but everyone looks better with makeup.

A missionary stopped me once in the street. Young man, blond crew cut. Extremely American, with a name like Tristan. And he said not what he had been planning to say but what he had thought when he saw me, striding down the street with a bag of books over my shoulder in my big dungarees and my hair held up by a red ribbon.

Ma'am, has anyone ever told you how lovely you are?

And I laughed and said,

Yes. Many, many men.

Many men? he said, confused.

Many.

And he frowned as if God had done him wrong by letting other men get there first.

Do you have any questions about heaven? he asked me.

No need to ask how to get there. I know the way to my own front door.

A different missionary (I know, it's hard to believe) walked past me on a train in his cassock and then doubled back on himself. I was studying for my GCSEs and he knelt beside my seat and placed a silver medallion of the Madonna on my open notebook.

You're going places, he said. You keep studying and she'll make sure of it.

I lost that necklace at a festival, the same day I lost my virginity to my boyfriend. It hurt so much I couldn't walk straight after. Maybe she left. Maybe she'd seen all she needed to see – me, flat on my back in a tent, grinning with pain over a rugby player's shoulder. Look who made it here all the way from Babylon. Maybe if you put the two men of God together, you get the truth. I am going places, and it's for only one reason.

Do you know what my least favourite thing about the Madonna/Whore complex is? Two Shot says, her shoulders bare and gold in the light from the candles in our favourite dive bar. Whisky glasses everywhere. The pool cue, for the moment, leaning unused on the wall.

What? I say.

That you have to fucking choose one.

In the stories about sirens, I always want to be a sailor, like my father. I don't want to be one of the naked women swimming in the water, not until they are licking men's bones with their rough tongues. One of my favourite books growing up was a book about a girl who is put on a boat as a kind of irritating, sentient cargo, shipped from America to England to stay with a family who will turn her into a lady. I can't remember the name of the book, but I read it over and over. She ends up becoming the captain; the cover is a picture of her hanging off the rigging in a tattered blue dress. She talks about how her feet get rough and calloused and how she could scamper to the crow's-nest in under a minute. You know that feeling you get when you watch a bird diving off a building? When they tuck their wings in and fall, your heart falls with them. I feel like that when I look at masts.

I used to run around barefoot to get my feet ready to captain a ship. I ran like that until I ran too fast on the wooden dock where my father's boat was moored and I got a splinter of wood all the way through my foot.

Why didn't you have shoes on? he asked me after he'd pulled the piece of wood from my foot and taken me to get a tetanus shot. He'd wrapped me in one of his jackets and put me next to my sister on the red leather bench seat of the truck.

I want to be a captain, I said.

OK, he said. You can be. You be the skipper, I'll be the cabin boy.

When my sister and I were growing up, my family called her the smart one. I was the beautiful one. You have to be smart to be a captain. Women are nothing but bad luck on the sea. But I used to lean down when our boat was going so fast it was lying on its side like a dog who wants to have its belly scratched, and trail my hand in the water. I used to jump off the back into the black, even though I was scared.

When I imagine being on the sea, I imagine standing on the deck with my hands crossed behind my back, listening. The whistle of the watch makes my heart dip. Cold sound in cold air. I blow smoke rings with the fog. I am wearing a coat with the collar turned up and the men touch their forelocks with respect, and I am loved and brave, and I have killed men above decks, never in the water. I curl my lip at the sirens who look a lot like me. I am brave. I am loved. I am my father's daughter.

But I know it isn't that simple. I am the ocean around the ship. I am the captain and the siren who kills him. I am the crabs eating old flesh. I am a night too dangerous to be sailed in.

I am the ocean around the ship.

~

Don't you want to talk about it? Two Shot asked.

Not really, I said.

Hero, Tex said. Come on.

It was so stupid.

I doubt that, she said.

I told them,

The argument started because I was making coffee.

Don't. You came over, turned down the heat. *It doesn't need to be that hot.*

What is your problem?

I don't have one, you said. You walked out of the kitchen. I followed you.

You know, if I've done something wrong, or if you need some space, tell me, I said. I don't want to spend all morning playing 'guess what's wrong with my boyfriend'.

Oh, fuck off, you said.

Don't fucking talk to me like that.

Yeah, you know what, I do want some space, you said.

Well, then say that, I said.

I just did, you said.

Why does it have to get to this point? Why do we have to be shouting at each other before we figure anything out? Why can't we talk about stuff?

Oh, you want to talk about stuff? you said, slamming your laptop shut.

How about the fact that I fucking asked you to marry me a

month ago and you keep changing your mind and you won't tell me why?

I told you, I said, I want some time to think about it. I don't know if I'm ready.

Why not? you said. *This is what people in love do, darling. They get married, they have kids. You don't have to act like it's such a fucking imposition.*

It isn't like that for me, I said. I don't want to be a wife or a mum – I want to be a person.

Oh my God, you are a person, you said, shouting now, standing up. *You're my favourite person. And what do you think makes you so special? Why isn't it like that for you?*

I'm your favourite person for now, I said, until I don't look like this any more and you have an affair with someone ten years younger than us or you fucking die.

That's insane, you said. *When we have these conversations, it's like you can't see me. It's like you're arguing with hundreds of other people.*

I'm sorry that I have fucking baggage, I shouted. It's not my fault that everyone I've ever dated has gone out of their way to try to ruin my fucking life.

Wow, you said. *That's really nice, Hero.*

I don't mean you. I just – do you know any happy marriages? Any? Look at your fucking parents – they got married and then found out they couldn't be in the same room. Look at mine! That's supposed to be this grand love story and it was so hard all the time.

We at least should try, you said. *It will still be us. I'm not going to marry you and suddenly expect you to turn into some housewife. I want to marry you because I love you.* You ran your hands through your hair. *It just doesn't feel that compli-cated to me.*

I looked out the window. A magpie, sitting on the railing. Staring me right in the eye. Horror, sitting outside my house like a three-headed dog.

I don't know that I can be anybody's wife, I said. It's not specific to you. If I was going to spend the rest of my life with anyone, I said, looking at you, you know it would be you.

～

I was walking away from the front of your restaurant when someone said,

Hero.

The restaurant had looked empty from the outside. All the doors ajar. A curtain fluttering at the corner of an open window. I had eaten a strawberry from the window boxes you planted and felt like a thief. Crushed it against the roof of my mouth in one starving breath.

It looks friendly, I'd said, the first time I came for dinner and you brought each dish to my table. Hearing the other chefs' laughter when you came back, and smiling, knowing they were teasing you. I came on my own and read my book and smiled so hard every time I saw you that my face hurt afterwards.

Sorry, I said, wiping my red fingers on my jeans. I didn't think anyone would be here, or, I thought you'd all be having a break out back or . . .

Your boss smiled. Leant his weight on one leg and raised an eyebrow.

. . . something. I didn't think you would catch me stealing strawberries.

They're there to be eaten, he said.

He has a tattoo of a pig on his arm. I'd asked him once, at a party,

Why the pig?

He'd shrugged.

I like pigs.

OK, I'd laughed. It's just a little . . .

He'd been stretched out on the couch, stoned, his arms spread out along on the top of the upholstery. His black T-shirt riding up on one side. The tightness of the skin around the hipbone. The smooth hollow beneath it.

It's a little what?

It's just a little cheffy, I said.

You think? What about the earring?

I like the earring. You look like a pirate.

I'll keep it then, he said.

I brushed my fingers over the pig's snout.

He's nice. He's kind of jolly. You know, sailors used to get pigs and chickens tattooed on their feet.

Oh, yeah? Why's that?

I'd come straight from work and was wearing jeans and a thin white T-shirt with a stain on the bottom left flank. Truffle oil. I could smell it. I wasn't wearing a bra and my hair was held up by a pen and I felt like something easy to eat and gone in one bite. The inside of my legs slick with sweat. Butter, gliding across the surface of a pan.

The livestock used to be kept in these wooden crates and so when the boats went down, the crates were the only things that floated. They thought that if they had a pig or a chicken on their leg it would keep them safe in a shipwreck.

One dark curl falling into his face.

You have any?

Yeah, a couple. A terrible one I got for an ex-boyfriend.

No way – show me.

Oh God, no, it's so bad.

Is it his name? he asked, squinting at my side.

Yeah, how'd you guess that?

I didn't. Your shirt is so thin that I can see through it, he said, gesturing towards my ribcage with his beer. His fingers wrapped around the neck of it.

Oh, I laughed.

Do you think you'll get any more?

I think so. I want 'HOLD FAST' on fingers like a—

Sailor.

Like a sailor, yeah.

Is there something in particular, he'd asked me, opening another beer and putting it into my hand, that you're scared you'll let go of?

How are you? I asked. How's work?

Good. It's busy, but lots of people are out of town for the summer, so not too bad. You?

A leaf shuddered down the pavement, blown by a summertime wind. What is going to happen can be seen. Earlier, when I walked under a fig tree, the air smelt like figs and even though I could see that they weren't ready to be eaten yet, I could already taste them.

Yeah, the same, I said. The owners are away so it's a lot of ordering wine and trying to get receipts to make sense.

He smiled.

I meant more like, how are you?

He had eased his foot out of his clog and was resting it on top of his other foot. The arch of his sock damp with sweat.

I'm fine.

Yeah? he asked.

A bus whooshed by. The squeal of a bicycle wheel.

Listen, he said, running a hand through his hysterical, fainting curls, looking over his shoulder at the façade of the restaurant, the ropes in his neck tightening as he does, I'm actually finished now. I need to get changed, obviously, he said, gesturing to the belt of oil on his apron where he must have leant his weight against the counter, because I smell like beef fat, and I need to brief the guys on dinner, but do you want to do something? Like, get something to eat? And talk?

Your apartment is nice, I said.

He had his back to me, standing at the stove. His kitchen walls were painted orange and there were twinkle lights strung over the top of the cabinets. I was sitting on a stool, resting my elbows on the kitchen island that separated the kitchen from the living room.

Thanks, he said, smiling over his shoulder. I bought it when I broke up with my ex.

How long ago was that?

Five years ago.

Were you together for a long time?

Yeah, we were together for eight years. I met her when I was twenty-three, at culinary school.

She was a chef?

She runs a restaurant in Oslo now.

That's really cool.

She is very cool.

He wore a black T-shirt and black straight-cut jeans. He was barefoot. Steam plumed up from the stove. He looked like a blacksmith. The heat, the steam. The film of sweat on the back of his neck.

He filled up my glass.

It's so good, the wine. It tastes like honey.

Yeah. I thought it would work with the food.

He spilt a little of the wine as he poured it. He wiped it up with his finger and licked it clean. The rough fabric of his jeans brushed against my leg.

What are we having?

We're having pork marinated in honey and five spice and tamarind. We're having rice, made by my friend – he gestured to a rice cooker – and steamed vegetables with a chilli ginger dipping sauce.

Wow, I said.

I hope you're hungry.

Always, I lied. Do you normally cook like this after work?

He laughed.

Never. If you look in my bin, you will see a lot of McDonald's wrappers. I only cook like this when I'm trying to impress somebody.

Oh, it's very impressive.

He smiled. The fat spat in the pan. He moved away to flip it. Placed his hand on my knee as he walked past as if the space was tight enough to demand it.

Do you cook much? he asked.

No, not at all. Like, I can cook. But he – living with a chef, you know. He cooks a lot more than me.

What have you been eating this week?

A whole lot of nothing, I said.

He looked right at me.

He's a great chef, he said, he's really imaginative and ambitious. I love that kid.

Can I ask you a question?

Sure, he said.

Why did you and your ex break up?

Oh God, he laughed. Ask me after I've had more wine.

Was it your fault?

What do you think? he said.

I don't think about you when we fuck. I think about you, for a second, when there is a pause in the music and he gets up to change the record.

Do you remember that Valentine's Day when we came back from dinner and you carried me up the stairs? There was no reason to – you just did it because it was romantic. We kissed like teenagers and when you put on the radio, they were playing 'Lady in Red' and we danced in our tiny kitchen, my face tucked into your neck. My stockinged feet on our cheap linoleum. When the song ended and we looked at each other, we had both teared up and then we couldn't stop laughing at how fucking tragic it is to cry to 'Lady in Red'.

You aren't even wearing red, you said, *that's the most embarrassing bit. Fuck,* you laughed. *I'm so in love with you.*

He turns round and grins. He dances a couple of beats towards me, laughs at himself. Takes off his apron in one smooth movement and throws it on to the couch. A metronome starts in the small of my back. I say,

I should go.

Men like this hate being told what to do. He says,

Let's have another drink.

And I say,

Yes.

This makes him feel like he is leading me to destruction and this reminds me that I like to be destroyed. After that, it is a matter of him asking me,

What do you want to drink?

And me saying,

Make yourself something and I'll have a sip.

An old and lazy trick. I've been using it to get men to kiss me since I was sixteen. The sound in my ears roaring like waves, crashing around the base of my cursed rock. He pours a sweet golden wine into a small glass etched with flowers. He holds it between two fingers, as if he is having tea with a doll. He offers it to me. I shake my head and say,

You first.

Like it could be poisoned. Fairy food. The taste of pomegranate as the gates of hell click gently closed behind you. He takes a drink and puts it down. I lean forward to run my tongue along his bottom lip, nothing else touching, the only part of me on him my tongue, him closing his eyes thinking it is happening now, him closing his eyes expecting the rest, braced for the weight, me already on the way back down into my chair, creating a distance that has now become ungovernable. When I say,

You taste good,

I am not thinking of you.

I don't think of you when he pulls my chair away from the table and kneels down in front of me and slides his arm between my legs to open them. I don't think of you when he says I taste like sea water and I see it washed over his chin. I don't think of you when I am on top of him, gripping his throat with my hand, getting wetter because my hand is so small against the shingled rough of his neck and him smiling because I am not strong enough to effectively constrict his oxygen flow. I am not thinking of you when I put his earring in my mouth. I am not thinking of you when he leaves me lying face down on his bed so that he can unhook the mirror from the bedroom wall, prop it on the floor, pick me up and place me on my knees in front of it. The light harsh and white, obscene in its clinicality. Carpet screaming in time on my elbows. When I make eye contact with first him in the mirror and then myself, I am thinking not where are you. I am thinking, there I am.

I do think about you afterwards, when he stands up to wash himself and he kisses me once, gently on the mouth and

I am surprised by the sweetness of the gesture. I go cold when I recognise it for what it is. Reflexive. A habit formed from a decade of loving someone else. Like a photograph, with a face cut out and a heart-shaped hole where the person used to be. The only thing left is the love.

It got light in the weak, jaundiced way of early morning. The bed was cold. It smelt like coffee and there was the sound of a spoon, clinking against something, a drawer being opened and then shut.

Are you OK? he asked when I walked into the kitchen.

I think so.

How's your head?

Not great, I said.

You haven't slept enough, he said. Go back to bed.

He was wearing a branded T-shirt from the restaurant – you have the same one – and boxers. His hair tousled as if a loving aunt had just removed her hand from it. Why do men always look like little boys in the morning? Another cruel enchantment to stop you from leaving.

I don't think I'd be able to sleep, I said.

If you're cold there's a blanket over on that couch, he said, gesturing with his head. Sit down, I'll bring you a coffee.

You're freaking out, aren't you? he said.

Yeah, I said. Breathing through my nose. I am freaking out a little bit.

Because we slept together and you're scared to tell him?

Yeah, mostly that.

What else?

I leant my elbows on his open window ledge and hung my head out. A drunk girl desperate for air in the back of a moving vehicle.

I feel kind of disappointed, I said.

Thanks, he laughed.

Not like that. I mean, I did think you were too good looking to be good in bed.

I'm not that good looking, he said, blowing smoke out of the window.

Shut up.

He passed me his lit cigarette.

I thought I would do it and feel guilty. And I do. But it also felt amazing.

I don't look at him when I'm talking. I don't want to know whether he is smiling or not.

I didn't think that I would feel so myself. I guess I thought it would feel, the whole time, like lying. But it didn't feel like lying at all. You know?

I know, he said. He looked at the ceiling. With me and my ex-girlfriend we met when we were really young, and while we were together we changed so much. But then, in other ways, we didn't change at all. We were really in love. We worked a lot, and whenever we had a day off we would lie in bed all morning and have sex and drink coffee and then get up and wander to a friend's bar somewhere and play cards or do the crossword.

That sounds nice, I said.

It was special. Every morning when I woke up with her I was excited to be there. It was – yeah – it was crazy. Every time she got home from work I couldn't wait for her to come through the door. I used to wait in the hallway, around the time that she was coming home, and like listen at the door to see if I could hear her footsteps in the hallway and then I'd have to run away so she didn't find out I was just standing there, waiting for her to come home. It's not like we weren't happy – we were happy; I was fucking obsessed with her. It was just that I wanted to know what the other options were, you know? I could see my whole life in front of me. We knew we wanted kids, we knew we wanted to get married, we wanted to live in the city as long as we could and then move to the coast and open up a seafood bar called The Limpet. It wasn't that I didn't want it, but I wanted other things too. And then I, he inhaled, his chest rising and his shirt shyly going with it, that line of exposed skin, slept with someone else. It was someone I worked with and I fucked her at work, after everybody else had gone home.

Were you drunk?

No, he said. I planned it. I knew she was on a close with me that night and I knew the spots that the CCTV didn't pick up. I can't sit here and say I was drunk, I had no idea what I was doing. It was definitely premeditated. Even just telling the story now, he said, I can remember the feeling of the cement floor on my hands. It was cold. I put a tea towel behind her head so she didn't like, get a concussion or something.

How did you tell your ex?

I didn't tell her for a couple of weeks. I would look at her and think about saying it and I – he sighed – couldn't do it. But she used to come into work all the time and once I saw her chatting to the girl I'd slept with and I felt like I was going to throw up or faint or something. So I told her that night when we got home. She thought I was joking. She was so surprised that she honestly thought I was joking for probably the first five minutes of the conversation. She was still saying, that isn't funny, when she started crying. And then she left and moved back to Norway to be with her family and we sold our house and she's not spoken to me since.

Fucking hell, I said.

Yeah. But it suits me better, being like this. I would've been a terrible husband. I like it more in some ways, being alone, being able to do what I want and not having to check with somebody. I feel like I'm such a lone wolf person, you know?

You sound, I said laughing, like such an asshole.

Baby, he said, so do you.

He said, while I am gathering my things and running a hairbrush (owner unknown) through my hair,

You're going to be fine, you two.

What? I said, standing in his bedroom. The damp bed.

You two. It's obvious, it always has been.

That's an insane thing to say. Why did we do this if you thought that?

He smiled, sitting in an armchair by the window. I was reminded that he is ten years older than me.

I wanted to. And I thought it would make you feel better.

So this has been like charity for you?

That's not what I said. I've always wanted to fuck you, you know that. But I knew you were going to do something like this the first time I met you. You're like me. You have one eye on the door. I felt like it would be good for you to really feel what it's like to pick the other option. I won't tell him, he added. He'll never find out.

I ran out the front door. I wanted to be home so badly. When I got through the door to our apartment I felt exactly the same. I still wanted to go home. After my father died, we used to say to our dog,

Where's dad?

And he would run around the house looking for him.

~

Have you heard the one about the woman who lived at the edge of the wood? I'm sure you have, but I'll tell it again.

There's a lesson to learn and it's worth noting down: any man is better than none at all, and if you have none at all then you may as well be dead, and if you don't agree we'll kill you.

Once upon a time an old woman lived at the edge of the wood. She had been young once, everyone agreed on that, but now she wasn't and she talked to herself and talked to the bees that lived in the hive under the arbutus tree next to her cottage. There are details that are not important. Why she never married (write this down: never smile at a man if you know what's good for you), why she preferred the company of bees to people (write this down: everything about you is something to be judged), why the village decided to turn on her that winter (write this down: obedience is the price of survival).

All of these things added up to an autumn when the harvest rotted on the stalk and tree, and then a winter when babies froze to death in their cots, and the only thing out of the ordinary in the whole village, the only thing that wasn't quite right, was the woman who lived at the edge of the wood. So they killed her.

It was something to do, after all. And when the next harvest was good they felt pleased at their ability to spot rot on the root, as it were. Their ability to recognise when small deeds deserve big punishments.

Look at that young woman, putting flowers on the stone over the bones of the woman who lived on the edge. She's wiping birdshit off the rock. She's lifting her goldilocks hair from her long thin neck. She's twisting it up with a ringless hand.

She's opening the door of the house at the edge of the wood.

Day Six

or

The Book of the Dead

The day before you were due to come back, I went to my mother's house. I smelt like someone else and it was infecting the apartment. Our gods, angry at the way I dirtied the temple. I was scared of touching anything in case I left behind ugly marks.

My mother hugged me hard when I walked through the door. She said,

Oh, darling.

I've been taller than her since I was fourteen. She cupped my face in her hand.

I'll make a cup of tea, she said. She took my bag.

Mum, I asked, what did you like about your first husband?

She looked up from her phone, her glasses perched right at the end of her nose.

He was tall, she said.

I laughed. My feet were draped over the arm of the sofa and every now and then she rubbed one of them absent-mindedly.

Anything else?

I can't remember. But I know we had fun.

And why did you leave him? What did you guys fight about?

The window is open and we can hear her neighbours crunching around their sad gravel garden. They have a habit of peering through the fence. I liked that Mum didn't lower her voice when she said,

I felt trapped. I couldn't be myself. But – she looked up at the light pooling on to the ceiling from our star slipping itself below the horizon – I don't remember any particularly bad fights. It's not like he was doing anything wrong. He wasn't a bad man.

She looked at me.

I can't believe that I was your age when we got divorced, she says.

~

As soon as you proposed, I told my mother. She came up to visit us and didn't ask about it until you'd left the balcony and gone inside to cook.

Are you feeling OK?

Sure.

You are so like me, she said.

Did you like being married all those times?

Don't say it like that. You make it sound like I've been married ten times.

You've practically been married three times.

I've been married twice.

And engaged three times.

She laughed. She brushed her hair out of her face and leant back like me.

I hated it, she said. I absolutely hated it.

Why? I asked, even though I had heard this story so many times I could tell it as my own.

I don't think I should ever have got married. I loved your dad, she said. I did. But I shouldn't have married him. I didn't want to be anybody's wife.

Did I ever tell you that my mother wore black when she married my father? Almost like she knew.

What's your hesitation? my mum asked me. Do you love him?

I laughed at the silliness of it.

Yes.

Then, what? she asked.

I'm not sure that it's enough. I'm not sure it will be enough for me.

She smiled at me. Ran her thumb over my knuckles.

No, she said. It never was for me.

My father brought my mother into his office. He didn't have a job, he was retired, but he had an office. He pointed out the dust on his desk. My mother had probably just got home from a twelve-hour work day. She looked at the dust on his desk and wrote,

FUCK YOU,

in it and walked away.

She still did all the cleaning. And all the cooking. When she asked why he wouldn't help, my father replied,

You've got two daughters, don't you?

It's a trap, my mother says. You think you're free, and then you get married. Then, you think it's tolerable so you have a baby. And then it's – she spreads her hands out – over.

Before you asked me, I would be doing something mundane like cutting vegetables or having a shower and I would think,

Nobody is ever going to want to marry me.

It would make me feel like a child, lost in a supermarket. Suddenly very willing to be good.

My mother used to say that I would get married young. We were all surprised when my sister won that race, not because she isn't lovely, but because I am reckless. I run, laughing, into darkened woods. I dare the wind to come and get me. I used to wear a shark tooth around my neck as if to say,

DANGER: DO NOT SWIM IN THESE WATERS. When my mother got married for the first time at nineteen, she wore a beautiful, long-sleeved dress. Her hair cropped very short. In the pictures, she's impish. She looks like she has pulled off an excellent trick. When she got divorced at twenty-six, she went back to the house she grew up in with a suitcase full of her belongings. Her husband showed up with a bouquet of flowers and her father said,

Well, it's all right then. You'll be going back, I expect.

She just ran. She let him have everything. The cottage. The dog. The car.

Years later, when I was in my mid-teens, her first husband got her mobile number off her dad. He texted her and they went for a drink.

Would it have been so bad, he said, halfway through his second rum and Coke, if we had stayed together?

She won't tell me if they kissed that night. He texts her once a year, on their anniversary.

Be careful, my mother's friend says, that you don't marry somebody else's husband. It ruins lives, that sort of thing.

My mother says, of her friends' loveless marriages,

Nobody wins.

My mother says the same thing of her friends' brutal divorces, the new, soulless apartments, the family albums, divided and meaningless without the story that comes with them, the pictures of people who loved each other and wanted to do their best ending up for sale as curiosities at rainy flea markets.

~

I've been having horrible dreams. In them, I am already dead and I am watching myself decompose.

I asked you once what would happen if I got a residency and we had to move somewhere, somewhere you maybe didn't want to live.

We'd go, you said, not looking up from your book.

What if it was like, a writer's residency in Rome and you had a job in London?

Well, we'd have to evaluate it and see what was best.

Would you be OK with us living separately if we had to? Like, if it was best for our careers?

You looked up then and frowned.

No, you said. *Would you be?*

I paused before I said,

I don't know.

I think about the time I said to Two Shot,

I hate that I have to choose. I hate that I have to make all these compromises all the time. I want to be like a man. I want everything.

If you had to choose between him and your career, which would you choose? Two Shot asked me.

I don't want to choose, I said.

She raised her eyebrows.

And I want a million dollars, she said.

In the dreams that I keep having, I am walking through a wood. It is dark and wet. I can feel the wetness seeping into my boots as I trudge along without any idea where I am going. As soon as I have the thought that I don't know where I'm heading, I can hear the crunching of bones, and I walk towards it. The woods are a watercolour blur of black and green and I am too scared to look at them closely in case they turn out to be something different. I walk for what feels like hours. I am tired. Every night I think that maybe when I get to where the sound is I will find you, deboning a chicken. Or gnawing on a rib, with sauce smeared around your chin like a child. Every night, I quicken my step at the thought. The woods bottom out into a clearing in a way that makes me teeter on the edge of the trees like I am teetering on the edge of freezing cold water. In the centre of the clearing, there are foxes, eating. They yip to each other. I smile. I love foxes. I run down the hill towards them thinking that maybe you are there and we are going to play.

When I see that it is me and that I am lying dead on the floor of the forest I reel backwards, but I am dreaming and so I can't run properly and the foxes squeal to each other and run around my ankles and rub their bloody little faces against my legs and I stare down at my naked white body, with neat chunks bitten out of the haunch and the thing that used to be my neck and is now a jowl, and I realise that you are absolutely nowhere to be found.

When I left home and then came back, people would ask me what the best part was. The weather, I would say. The feeling of waking up knowing it would be sunny. Listening to the sound of car horns in the morning and driving through a city in the dawn, watching people ease themselves into the day. When I think of those mornings, I think of bougainvillaea tumbling off balconies. The taste of cold black coffee. Pastry filled with cream falling apart on its way to my mouth. Light cloth fluttering around my knees and sticking to the small of my back. People said that it made sense, the running.

They said,

Well, of course she's with an older man. She doesn't have a dad.

Or,

The fucked-up girls are always the hottest.

Before we got together, I was going to go travelling when I finished my degree. I was going to go and write a book and drive down the road and breathe in the early morning air in huge mouthfuls. I visited one of the cities he took me to a couple of years after I left it. The first night I was there, I sat at a bar in a square paved with white marble and cried. I drank my Aperol Spritz between sobs. My friend said,

What's wrong? Do you miss him?

And I said,

No. I miss me.

I spent the month we were there looking for my eighteen-year-old self. I thought I would see her, walking past the market with her new sunglasses on, picking her way through puddles in her high-heeled sandals. I can't wear heels any more. I broke my foot in that city, dancing. Near the end of our trip I realised why I wanted to find her so much. I figured out why I wanted to see her on her motorbike, a paperback tucked into the back pocket of her shorts. It was because she didn't exist any more. We killed her between us, me and him. I held her down and he placed the pillow over her mouth.

~

My dad almost died when I was in primary school. He got into a car accident in our white Toyota truck. The truck was totalled so we took it to a scrap yard, and every time we drove past in our new, bigger truck I would avert my eyes so I wouldn't have to see the place where something I loved went to die. Someone must have called the school to tell them he was in an accident and I remember my name being called over the PA system. I went, my light-up shoes flashing in the hallway, and they said,

Wait here for your sister,

but no one would tell me what was going on, so I ran around the halls looking for her. She went to the office and couldn't find me and we both ran round and round the school until we bumped into each other outside her Third Grade classroom. Sloppily coloured card turkeys taped up against the classroom door. They let us play skittles in the gym. They got all the fun equipment out and the headmaster came and played with us. He was a kind man; he pushed kids on the swings at recess. I kept asking,

Where's my dad?

I knew something was wrong. The feeling crept up on me. In the writing business, we call that foreshadowing.

The double gym doors swinging open with a clunk and my dad walking in with his arms already outstretched. The squeak of light-up gym shoes on a shiny gym floor.

Do you remember when I came home from work that time and shouted at you? I still had my waitress apron on, full of crumpled receipts and pen ink. I stood in the doorway and threw my bag on the couch, and when you said,

How was your day?

I said,

Why the fuck haven't you tidied up? It's so fucking annoying to be at work all day and find the flat in a fucking state.

You cried. You said,

I feel like nothing I do is ever good enough for you.

You almost died when you were in primary school. A truck hit you.

When I used to walk to school, I would walk past the spot where I'd got hit and there was a bloodstain on the pavement, you said.

Gross, I said.

Yeah, you said. *It always made me feel weird. It always made me feel like I'd barely escaped.*

You were cycling to school. When the driver got out, you lay on the pavement and said,

I'm sorry. I'm so sorry,

because you were afraid that you had made his life diffi-cult. I can imagine your mum getting the call that you were in hospital. I know the calculations she will have made as she slammed the door shut and ran down the road as hard as she could. Can I live without him? I promise, if he's OK, I'll never be ungrateful again. I promise, if he's OK, I'll love him as much as I can.

My mother used to come home from work and find my father in the bath, drinking a glass of wine. He would tell

her about his day, and ask her what we were having for
dinner. If she said, Soup,

or,

Caesar salad,

he would say,

No, really, what are we having for dinner?

Or,

Are you making it all from scratch?

She did not tell him any more about her male friends
who came into the library where she worked and talked to
her about books because if she did, he said,

Married women don't behave like that.

Like what? she demanded, still holding her work bag in
the bathroom doorway.

Married women don't do that, he said.

On one of my father's bad days, he requested the records
from the phone company. He looked for numbers he didn't
recognise, and asked my sister and me if we knew who
they belonged to. He asked who my mother had been calling
and we said we didn't know, and my sister cried because
she felt these things more than I did.

We went to Venice when I was about eleven. We found out
later that my dad already had tumours, he just didn't have
any symptoms yet. He carried those tumours around Europe.
They sat with us in the BMW we hired, an impractical car

for taking Alpine bends at the ready-for-death speed my father liked to drive. But the backseat was so big that I could sleep stretched out without my head or toes bumping the grey plastic of the doors. We sang Jerry Lee Lewis songs as we drove through Switzerland. My dad bought me a dirndl in Germany, and the second we crossed the Italian border I begged him to pull over so I could change my clothes in a public toilet by the side of the road. Thin, cold air and sleek black cars whooshing by. I was taking sewing classes back home and I put on a turquoise shorts-and-top set that I made myself. It was covered in tie-dye fish. I swanned back to the car, my dirndl tucked under my arm and my dad said,

If I didn't know any better I'd think you were Italian.

It was hot in Venice that day. The water was begging and I lingered by the sides of canals, dipping my hand in them. Watching the small transparent fish giggle in the sun. We didn't sightsee. Let's get lost, my dad said, after we had wandered into St Mark's Square and promptly wandered back out. I still don't sightsee. I am nothing but the things my parents did and didn't do. The alleyways looked like baked sponge cake. Yellow and warm, and something soft about the way they ran around the buildings, desperate to stay close to that topaz water. Cold coins being put into my palm, being allowed to go round the corner from where my father was buying gifts for my mother, to fetch us gelato.

Holding the coins so hard in my hand that I had battlements ridged into my palm when I finally slid them on to the plastic counter.

My father walked with his big camera slung around his neck, which smelt like sunscreen. He had sandwiches wrapped up in kitchen roll in the pockets of his cargo shorts because they'll charge you an arm and a leg for a slice of pizza – and I'm not paying for lunch out when we've got all this breakfast food I've already paid for. Now when I am in old, hot cities, I stroll and I linger and I run my fingers over the pockmarked stones and wonder what it would be like to be known by them. I consider what it would feel like to know the local clocktower intimately, to wave to it every morning. Then, I ran everywhere. I careered around street corners and waited, panting, for my dad and sister to catch up.

He spent two hours in a lace shop, picking gifts for my mother. I sat by the edge of the canal with my gelato and dangled my feet in the water and heard his voice drifting out of the shop. He called my sister in to try clothes on and he stood back and shook his head and said no, that isn't quite right, I want something that will bring out her skin tone. He had put his camera down on a table covered with lace doilies. He was a big man and he stepped carefully around mannequins. He paused to run his hands over thin nightgowns and blouses. He bought my mum a jacket that she never ever wears. The woman behind the till sighed when he laid it on the counter in front of her. She watched him walk out holding my hand. She watched him until we rounded the corner and disappeared.

~

My mother decided we should go out for dinner. To distract us, she said, and so we went to a restaurant downtown that she takes me to whenever I come home for the weekend. It was so humid that I had the feeling of swimming at a rock beach after the tide has come up. There are spots where the water is warm because it is sitting over a slab of sandstone which, having baked all day in the light, breathes the sun out into the water slowly, heating it from the bottom up. Then, there are other spots where it is suddenly deep and you are plunged into cold. The shock of it, because the surface of the water looks exactly the same.

The air smelt like hot road. It made me feel feverish and dizzy. Other people's scents staying longer in the air, trapped by the humidity. The town smelt like Lynx and vanilla and the first perfume I ever bought. Vera Wang Princess. It came with a scented body glitter that I wore to family Christmas parties. I can't afford perfume now. I crush lemon leaves against my throat and hope for the best.

Do you ever get bored, I asked her, living in a town like this?

I like it here, Mum said. We are drinking matching proseccos.

You've never really lived in a city, have you? I asked.

Yes I have, when I first lived with your dad, when we moved to Vancouver.

Did you like it?

I loved it, she said. She has grown her hair out after years of having it monk short. At night, she pulls handfuls of gold pins from it. Like needles out of a fairy-tale haystack.

You weren't scared or overwhelmed?

Oh, yes. Yes, I was. I don't know if I would do the same thing, given the chance all over again.

I frown.

Be with Dad?

She shook her head.

Leave my family behind and be away from my mum and dad for so long. But it was the making of me. I always felt, before I met your father and moved away, and before everything happened with him being ill, that I was quite lightweight really. A lightweight person.

In what way? I said, and I am aware that I am asking questions like an anthropologist: why and how and when. I am looking for the tell in my genes. Where is the twist in the arching spiral that makes me a goodbye girl?

I don't know, I just felt it. When I moved away with him, my life was so different overnight. We used to shut up the shop and go down the block to this local Mexican restaurant we liked. We would have a beer and get some food. Then we would go back to the flat and dance.

You and Dad?

Mm, we danced. Your dad was always doing these things to make me laugh: funny dance moves, making a fool of himself. I remember laughing a lot.

Did you kiss?

Of course, she smiled.

You were all over each other, I said, completing the memory.

Yes, we were. And then I would decide to make a cake or bake cookies and we'd stay up late. It was so different. I'd been so sick before I met Dad, so ill that I'd had to have a—

Blood transfusion, I said. I know the story.

A blood transfusion, she said. She took a sip of her drink. Her hands, they are sun-spotted all over. Looking at them these days makes my chest hurt. Don't go. When I hold my niece, fingers splayed strong and wide across her back or around her stomach, I see my mother's hands, as if they have been hewn off and attached to the end of my arms.

When I met your father, it all went away. I was fine, I got better. I know he wasn't easy, but he was the making of me. He was so difficult that when he died, I almost felt like I had been primed for his death by being with him.

I found an interview that I did with Dad, I said, that I think I must have done in Italy. It's written on these loose pieces of notepaper with a Commedia dell'arte clown on them. I asked him questions like his favourite colour.

Black, she said.

His favourite song, and his favourite memory.

She was watching the people on the street, her elbow propped up on the windowsill. This restaurant has huge windows that they open up in the summer so that the bar seems to bleed out on to the road. When we came in, she asked me,

Do you think they'll let us have one of those tables? And when we got one, she said,

This is really lovely,

three times.

She wears a ring my father bought her. I have put back on the ring you bought me. Twirling it around my finger as if rubbing it will magic you up. Treasure, stolen from someone who trusted you.

For his favourite memory, I said, he said: holding my wife in my arms.

She doesn't look at me, or change on the surface. Like the water, when you swim over an unexpected depth.

How does that make you feel? I asked.

I always knew he loved me, she said. In spite of everything else, I never once doubted that he loved me.

There were crab apples, sticky, burst and rotted on the

ground outside my mother's favourite restaurant. Something that could've been good for you is making a mess all over the sidewalk.

Why did you do it? my mother asked me.

My friend told me a story about a badger that lives in Norwegian woods. They know they can't really beat you, she said. They know you are bigger than them. What they do is bite your ankles, one after the other, to cripple you. They don't let go until they hear the bone break.

Are you going to tell him? my mother asked me.

They used to drown women to figure out whether they were witches or not. They tied women to chairs or, if chairs were not abundant in that part of the country, simply tied their ankles and wrists with twine and threw them into rivers and lakes and shallow, brackish ponds. You can drown in two inches of water. The idea was that if she was a witch, she would float and then you would fish her out and stone her to death or burn her. If she drowned, she was innocent. I wonder how many men stared at their wives or daughters or sisters, sinking slowly to the glassy bottom. I wonder if they felt guilty, or if guilt just didn't really come into it. After all, it was a tradition, and, as far as I know, nobody floated.

When I looked up at the sky, like it has ever done anything except make me feel small, she said,

I don't think that you have to tell him. Men have been doing this for centuries. Christ, she laughed, every man of my generation messed about before getting married. When I was twenty, my best friend's fiancé slept with someone else at his stag do and nobody was surprised. Darling, she said, reaching out to take my hand, do you have feelings for this other man?

No, I said. She rubbed my hand with her thumb.

Listen, she said. There are some things, she says, that you just don't tell your husband.

A couple, laughing at the next table. I want it so badly. I want you so badly I can't look at them.

I made a mistake, I said.

Yes, she said. You are allowed to.

~

There was a young man who lived in a small stone house on the edge of the sea. On stormy nights, the wind picked up the water and threw it as hard as it could at his kitchen window. In the morning, the windows were caked with savoury ice.

The man had a fishing boat called the *Flounder*, which he manned alone. He was not a solitary person by nature, although you would be forgiven for thinking he was, as it is often solitary men who make the best heroes. He had friends who loved him and who cheered in a good-natured way when he walked through the pub door after a long day skimming over the waves in a boat as cheerful as a well-tossed pebble. If you had seen him, as I have, lounging on a bar stool in his mac and his green knitted hat, you would have found yourself looking for too long. Dark curls on his head that make you feel thirsty, sitting in little whirlpools by his ears.

The man planted a vegetable garden behind his small stone house. He sat on his haunches and stared at the spot where seedlings were due to sprout. The sea turned into mist and slipped through the cracks under his door and lay, sighing, in his cupboards. No matter how long he hung his under-things in front of the fire, they were always damp. The sea kissed him in places she shouldn't have.

He was the most successful fisherman in the village. His boat groaned under the weight of so many slippery silver bodies. He had money to spare and he spent it on rounds in the pub, more seeds for his doomed garden. His friends rolled their eyes.

You need a woman, they said.

You need a feminine hand on that house.

The man smiled down at his pint. The barmaid rubbed the hard wood of the bar and watched him. When he went home that night, he lay in bed and ran his hand over the space beside him. It left a cold hollow in the white sheets.

One particularly cruel winter, the man woke after a storm. He sat up in his cream pyjamas and rubbed his eyes with his knuckles. His dog leapt on to the bed and rubbed her small face against his big one and whined to go out. The man moved slowly that morning, lumbering around the kitchen, lighting the stove, making coffee, pulling on his boots. When he opened the door the dog took off like fire on August grass and he trudged behind her, cradling his hot mug. He always found things on the coastline after a storm. A barely chipped enamel bowl. Yards and yards of rope. Sometimes, unopened bottles of rum that had floated gamely away from shipwrecks.

The dog ran back to him with things in her soft mouth. Normally, she brought him sticks to throw. Today, she ran back whimpering.

What is it? he asked, reaching down to rub her head. She pelted away and when she got to a spot where the sand gave way to a knoll of rocks, she paused and paced and whined and ran back to him, her black ears slicked back against her skull. The man stood still for a moment on the wet, grey sand. The slumped body of a seal. A white hand. He put his mug down gently on the nearest rock. A sand dipper skittered away in panic when he began to run. The cold air making tears stream down his cheeks.

Her skin was freezing cold. He put a blanket on the floor in front of the fire and laid her on it. He sat beside her. A nervous blue crab crawled out of her hair and tiptoed straight into the flames. The skin around her nipples was tight with cold.

The first thing she asked him was,
    Where is it?

She did try. He took her to the pub and watched her dance with his friends. She danced like water. She had all the terrifying promise of a blue-black sea. He walked through town with an arm around her shoulder as if that was the most natural thing in the world. Her selkie skin was safe in the chest at the bottom of the bed and for a while, they didn't talk about it. The key to the chest, unlike in other versions of this story, hung on a hook by the door. It was right there.

The selkie tried to make the garden grow. She spent the days he was at sea digging and sowing and getting down on her hands and knees to rescue worms from the cut and thrust of the spade. She asked the local wives for help.

They stood in a bemused semicircle around the edge of the sad, torn earth.

Am I sowing the seeds too close together? she asked from where she was squatting by her painfully ordered rows. One of the wives put a hand down to help her up.

No, she said. It should be working fine. She brushed dirt off the selkie's apron. Some people don't have green thumbs.

Is that bad? the woman asked.

It's bad for the things that grow, the wife said.

Oh, the woman said.

She made them tea and fed them gingerbread that the wives all said was lovely, but when they walked away the wife who had helped her stood at the crest of the hill and looked down at the cottage.

What is it? another one said.

She ain't made for that, she said. She'll be gone before winter.

Oh, come now, she loves him. Any fool can see it from a mile off. My George says they can't keep their hands off each other when they're down The Ship.

I don't doubt it, the wife said. At the bottom of the hill the selkie knelt in the dirt. Pulling up seedlings and looking at the shoreline.

There is a moment, not long after this, where the selkie walks out of the kitchen and stands behind the half-wall of the bedroom. She stares at the wall that separates her and the man and she rocks forwards and backwards, as if being hit by small waves. The man continues to talk. The man continues to say things that you and I and all grown-up people have burnt in our minds from memories that feel like stories. Stories about lives gone wrong. Stories about regret.

Can't you leave me alone for five minutes? I'm tired and I want to spend five minutes by myself without hearing about the fucking garden.

Before the selkie walked out of the kitchen she started to say,

I'm—

Don't, he said.

So, the woman stands there. Rocking her weight back and forth as if soothing a baby. She bites her lip and stares at the wall. Watching the seals swimming in the bay.

The next day, when the man goes to fish, the woman slips the key from the hook gently, like easing a hook out of a fish's shredded lip. She takes her skin out and sits on the cold flagstones of the kitchen. It spills over her lap. She sits and looks at it. A gull screams down the chimney. Sand skitters over the floor.

That morning, the woman let the skin slither on to the floor. By the door leant a shovel. That morning, she dug a grave in the garden. She diced her skin up with the sharp edge of the spade. The metal sparked as it hit the stones. The wives in the village paused in their housework. Several felt seasick and others cried suddenly, salt oozing from their bodies. The woman stood over the grave in the garden and cut her throat with a kitchen knife so that she would fall neatly into the hole.

In the version I was told, the selkie swims away. But I am determined to tell you the truth. She doesn't swim away because she has forgotten how to.

The garden grows well now, although the fisherman is not there to see it. He returned from that fishing trip full of apologies. The hole could be seen from the path that led to the cottage. Its edges fringed with seedlings. He looked at her cold back, flecked with brown dirt. He lay on his stomach so he could reach down and touch her tangled hair.

The fisherman walked down to the ocean with the dirt of the graveside on his smock and he was still crying when they found his body a week later. After they had dried him and covered up the parts of him shredded by barnacles, a wife pinched her friend. She pointed to the water running down his face.

He's crying, she says. He must have loved her.

I don't doubt it, she said.

Day Seven

or

Years gone by, and still

A normal night at home. Our playlist on the stereo and you making dinner. Me, sitting on the stool in the kitchen, watching you. You danced as you cooked, sang along under your breath.

Do you love me? I asked.

You looked at me.

Of course I love you, you said. You put the knife down. You kissed me on the forehead and held my face between your hands.

I love you even more than I did yesterday. And I loved you more yesterday than I did the day before.

~

Your great-grandparents met because your great-grandmother fell off her bicycle. She was cycling down the road in a chintz-patterned dress with her suitcase balanced on the handlebars. I like to think she was singing under her breath. The roads were gravelly and chequered with potholes like dangerous hopscotch, and she was caught up in the joy of being young and beautiful and alive, and her front wheel decided to teach her a lesson and that's how she ended up sitting on the gravel with her face bleeding through her fingers and on to her chintz-patterned dress. She looked at the red and looked at her underwear spilt all over the ground. And your great-grandfather ran out of the house and picked her up (after asking her if he could). He took her inside and wiped her face with a wet handkerchief. He gathered up her white cotton nightgowns and her cornflower-blue slips and only blushed a little when he shook the dirt from them.

My grandparents met because my grandmother fell off her bicycle. She was cycling down the road that led from the estate to the fields, with a basket balanced on her handlebars. She had hops to pick and boys to see, and the sun was shining and I guess she was caught up in being young and beautiful and alive and thinking how wonderful everything was, and that was when her bike chain decided to teach her a lesson and it fell off the chain ring, and that's how she ended up with a cut on her calf from the pedal, which didn't stop when the bike did. She got off and let the bike fall to the hot concrete with a clatter of apology. She looked at the red and looked at the basket, which was still in one piece. And my grandfather ran out of his house and hopped over the fence that separated his garden from the road. He asked if she was OK, he told her to sit on the kerb while he fixed the bike chain. He neatly picked up the basket and tied it to the handlebars with some twine that he had lying around, and he only blushed a little when she asked him his name.

~

Sometimes, I sit and imagine what it would be like if I didn't love you any more. I imagine my life. I would do the things I did before I loved you, back when I was wholly self-contained, like a beautifully organised boat. I could go anywhere. I had rooms inside me and also a place to dive from, into the ocean that looks endless but we all know has limited possibilities. Will you marry this man? Will you become a writer? Will you drown? There are only so many different things down there that you can be eaten by. In the version of us where I don't love you any more, I have fought my way out of you. I know the steps of this boxing match like it was beaten into me one punch at a time.

I thought that now that I'm more of a writer and less of a waitress I wouldn't need to love you any more. I eat what I want to eat and I cook it how I want to cook it (sorry). But last night, in the bath in my mother's house, I waited for you to come through the door and say,

Can I put my feet in?

But you didn't.

And this is what it will be like if I don't choose you, in the end.

The phone line crackles.

Are you going to tell him? Two Shot asks.

I don't know.

She sighs.

I think that if you don't, you're going to feel like the bad guy for ever. You don't want to carry that around – it's too heavy. I don't even think you should tell him for his sake, she says. I think you have to tell him for yours.

But, I said, so many bad guys end up really happy.

There is a noise, something soft being brushed against the phone. She's shaking her head.

I don't think you can charge your happiness to some-body else's account. It shouldn't cost them anything.

At dinner, at our favourite restaurant, I said,

I wonder if they do weddings here.

You looked at me carefully across a plate of langoustines, the speckled coral of them aggressive in the white room. They don't play any music at that place; you can hear the waitresses chatting to the chefs over the pass. You looked at me and your whole face softened.

I bet they do, you said.

You poured me another glass of wine. The bubbles in it hurled themselves to the top of the glass. When I brought it up to my face I felt them breaking free of the surface of the liquid and dancing before they wore themselves out into nothing and became another patch of air.

We could never afford it, I said.

You smiled.

We could make it work.

~

My mother has a friend who lived in a beautiful house that was exactly like a house in a fairy tale. It was tall and it ended in a weathervane that had a witch on a broom, spinning wildly in the wind. Raspberries leant drunkenly on each other at the bottom of the garden. The house smelt like incense and fresh coffee. There were always snacks. Flax muffins, warm, with heaps of butter.

My mother's friend wore her hair tied up with silk scarfs. She would wrap presents in these scarves, and so the books she gave smelt like Herbal Essences. She read, constantly. She had beautiful sons. She swore and drank whisky. When I saw her a few summers ago, she took me to a local art gallery, handed me a bottle of beer and introduced me to a famous novelist. She said,

Hero is a writer too.

She was married to a man who everybody loved. He washed his truck in the driveway on lazy afternoons and would hold the hose up in the sun so me and my sister and his boys could run through the rainbow, screaming with delight.

The woman was an artist. She had a shed at the bottom of the garden where she did her work. That was what I wanted. When I finally lived with someone I loved and who loved me, I thought, I would have an entire room just for me. It would be large. It would have big windows and gauze curtains, like the ones Daisy runs through in *Gatsby*. Heartbreak curtains. I would lock the door and then I would make good work, because in order to make good work, you have to do that, don't you? You have to choose.

The man waited until the boys were grown up before he left. According to the artist, she never saw it coming. He left like a mudslide. Days and days of rain that seeps into the earth until the ground would rather kill than stay put. A mountain moves itself.

He left and wouldn't tell her why. He lives down the road from the artist. When they bump into each other at the grocery store he doesn't even look at her. He walks past her in the dairy aisle to get to the mild Cheddar. Sometimes she sees him at local events. Barbecues. She sees him from across the way and when he laughs at a joke and takes a sip of his beer she feels like she's been punched right in the soft and crinkled bit of her stomach.

She doesn't make art any more.

My heart isn't in it, she says.

I guess she needed the boys, the husband. She needed a life.

~

When you used to go out and see your friends and come home late, I didn't worry that you had gone home with some woman with a softer voice than mine. I worried that you'd been hit by a car. I imagined you, twitching on the side of the road. A woman screams when she sees you, calls an ambulance. You die on the way to the hospital. Nobody tells me for hours. I spend half a day thinking you are going to come home, thinking we'll drink a beer and watch *My Neighbor Totoro*, like we planned. I tidy up our apartment while someone wheels your perfect body down to the morgue.

My father was not an easy man. This is something that people don't talk about in stories about death and grief. No one says, we miss him but he was a fucking nightmare. It makes people uncomfortable. If you say to someone: I'd rather my dad was alive, but if he was, I don't know if my parents would have stayed married, they'll say, oh my gosh no don't say that of course they would have. But people don't want to talk about dead parents at all. People want to believe that no one's parents die until everybody is in their fifties, and when you are already one parent down, it puts their fantasy in danger.

I'm so sorry that happened to you, but could we talk about something else? a friend said to me once.

It makes me too sad.

When he was dying, he no longer knew who he was or who I was, but he used the pitifully small amounts of energy he had trying to remember. He would sit on the sofa and stare up at me, waiting for me to tell him something that would make the situation sensible. I came home from school and stood in the living-room doorway in my uniform. The cords from his oxygen tank pooled like tangled jump ropes at my feet.

Mum, can I go to Cassie's house tomorrow after school?

Cassie's? Is her mum going to pick you up?

Yep, I said, licking my finger and rubbing pen off my hand.

Are you going to have dinner there?

She said she'd take us out for pizza.

Jane, my dad said. Trying, even then, to be a dad, to show that he knew things about my life. I didn't say anything back. I think about that all the time.

Yes, darling, Jane is Cassie's mum, my mother said. She laid her hand on my dad's arm.

There are things about the weeks before he died that my mind has cut out of my selfhood like redacted information in a transcript. I remember food people made us and left on the porch without a card because they knew the effort of saying thank you might kill one or all of us. I remember none of us answering the phone for weeks, the scream of it muting the helpful hum of the oxygen machine in the hall.

My dad was a boxer in his early twenties. I have no idea if he was any good. I imagine that he was; he was not a man who liked to lose. I never asked him about his fights – he might have been awful. But in my version (the short one) he is glorious. He is full of vitality and he is handsome, and when he wins he laughs like me. If I do something that scares me, like when I start writing each morning, or when I walk to an interview, I listen to the theme song from *Rocky*. I square my shoulders and throw a couple of jabs. He used to skip every morning in our basement, training for an unscheduled match with an unseen enemy. Our house was built into a stone cliff and I used to think it made so much sense, watching my sixty-year-old father skipping rope with a sweaty, contorted face in front of a sheer rock wall. When you are as little as I was, they seem equally as permanent. A cliff face and a father.

My mum told me that she has dreams that my dad comes back. He knocks on the door and he's alive but he's still sick. And in her dream, Mum says she realises two things.

1) She has to watch him die all over again.

2) He's going to start telling her what to do.

And even though she doesn't say this, I know that the reason the dream is, in fact, a nightmare isn't because he's going to cough and gasp and beg her to kill him one more time. But because as soon as he walks through the door, he asks her what's for dinner.

Lung cancer, when it gets bad, fills your lungs up with fluid. The fluid itself is full of cancer. A tide of death, lulled by a malicious moon. When it gets like that, you drown from the inside out. He must have been so angry to die that way. The boxer gets up until he can't any more. The captain goes down with the ship. It isn't right for a sailor to drown in their own bed. A week before he died, we planned to go sailing one last time. His friend, who last time he saw me cried

You're so grown up, your father would be so proud

was supposed to sail Dad's boat and we had packed a picnic. Before we walked out the door, Dad had a coughing fit and couldn't catch his breath. Everybody but him decided he wasn't well enough to go out, after all. And he looked out the window at the boats in the harbour and shook his head, and I think if I had to describe sadness I would describe it like that. A sailor drowns from the inside out while looking at the sea.

He said something to me when he was ill that I cannot quite remember. We lay in bed together. It was dark in the room and I think he had his dressing gown on in bed. My sister had given him a bear to tuck under his arm and I was in there too, snuggled into the place where the life comes from. And he said something like,

It doesn't have to be grand gestures. Just spending time together like this is nice.

But every time I try to remember, it gets harder. Because I know that I'm making it up. I did not know him well enough to imagine what he said.

You told me once that the job I was best suited to was pirate. My love of the sea. My ruthlessness.

My father, lying in bed with my mother and me, and thinking I was asleep, saying,

What do you think she'll be when she's older?

When my uncle, the closest person in the world to my father, was dying of lung failure and coughing and coughing, I told him I wanted to be a writer.

And he said,

Your father would've loved that. He would've loved it.

After my father died, we found his little black book. It was in the garage in a cardboard box full of other scrappy remnants of parts of his life that I never bothered to ask about. You asked me once about what my dad's university years were like and I had to say,

I don't know. I never asked him.

The little black book was heavy and worn in that way that full books are, as if the words are leaking and might puddle out around your feet. I feel that way about old classic paperbacks. I fear that if I open *The Odyssey* words like 'loss' and 'foretold' will end up staining my jeans like blackberry juice. Names and names and names, and none of them meaning anything to us. Pamela. Joanne. Dates: his America years, the years where he was married to other women. Names scattered throughout the years of those marriages, falling on to the page with the thud of a body falling into a grave. I didn't recognise the last name in the book until I realised that when my mother met my father she still had her first husband's name. What a thing to want. What a death sentence to say I will be you instead of me.

~

When the painter I loved finally left me, I didn't feel like a person any more. I noticed it most in the way that I saw everything that I did through his eyes. I would go out to eat with new friends and puzzle over the menu, trying to figure out what he would've picked. Alone, in my room, I listened to music that he liked. I grew my hair out long again because that's how it had been when we'd first met. I wanted to be as close as possible to his perfect version of me. I thought that if I did that, then eventually he would come back and treat me well. Which now, all these years later, looks insane when written down like that.

But I had just left school and had never experienced anything before, let alone the feeling of being driven down an empty highway by a man who is driving with one hand on the steering wheel so that he can hold your thigh with the other, like you are a stolen treasure that he wants to keep safe.

He told me I wasn't funny and got angry when I talked about the books I was reading. He didn't like it when I talked about writing or when I got excited about anything. I can still taste it. The feeling of walking into a dark room and knowing he wasn't there. The feeling of walking into a room and knowing that he wouldn't be happy to see me. I can remember sitting mutely next to him in the car, trying to figure out how to speak in a way that didn't annoy him or make him angry. I think sometimes that I am still trying to figure that out.

What's funny to me now is that I can't remember why I lost myself the way I did. I mean, I know he was older and I was a girl who had been told for most of her adolescence that she would eventually find a man who would put her in her place. I know I loved being a danger to myself. But I can't remember why I loved him so much. I must've had fun. Especially at the beginning, there must have been something that made me get down on my knees and beg for it the way that I did. It's all gone now. The odd memory of heat between my legs. My back against the linoleum floor of a hostel kitchen. Dancing at an all-night bar. The way he would look at me from across the room and dance towards me.

Even those things come with others. Rain falls when the heat breaks. I always worried that he only loved me because he could fuck me, and at the end we didn't even do that. When we went out dancing he would ignore me for long stretches of time and I would sidle up to him, the way you do to a wild animal that you don't want to scare off. It's strange that so much of how I remember that period of my life is me wrestling with myself instead of him. I was permanently engaged in suffocating myself with a pillow.

I read something recently about a woman who developed the tendency, after her mother died, of going into a trance-like state and acting out the hour or so after her mother's death.

This was particularly awful because in the hour after her mother's death, the daughter had feverishly attempted to bring her back to life. She performed CPR again and again and again on her mother's cooling corpse. Ribs cracking under the frenzy of miserable hands.

It was like that with me, after he left, except I was both of them: the mother and the daughter. And eventually, it worked, even though there were times where I thought it would kill me, that desperate resurrection. Bringing myself back into being after being eaten right down to the bone was the most tiring thing I have ever done. I am still tired. I don't think I could do it again.

Do you promise not to kill me if I promise not to kill you? I'm sorry I argue with him when you're standing in front of me. It's just, in certain lights. You are the only man who has ever been kind to me. You are the only man who loved me more the more he knew me. You are the only man I don't think I could live without. I have been so good at surviving it so far.

You be Hades and leave the door open. I'll be Cassandra and you'll listen when I speak. Give me the key to the chest with my skin. Watch me swimming from the shore, a cup of coffee in your hand. Laugh with delight at the way the ocean loves me. Rub me with a towel when I come back dripping. When you make me fairy food, please don't put anything in it that makes me forget who I am. Show me how to leave the castle. Say, I want you to stay. Help me hold up the bow made so heavy that only I can shoot it. When they ask about me, tell them the truth. Say, she was my hero.

I can't stop writing about you, because even when it seems like it's about you, it's about me. But I'll try to tell the story of us in the best way. This is a fiction. We are a myth. It stays alive as long as we keep telling it.

~

The world is slow and hot on my walk tonight. Your bus should be getting in soon and I walk a little faster. I don't want to be late. I can see a woman sitting in her car, counting rosary beads. What is she praying for? Maybe that the traffic speeds up. Maybe she has someone who never answers her calls. Water is pouring out of the wall of the underpass. The light hits it. It glints for a second, as I go past it, and the sun and I navigate around each other. No, you first. Waterfalls, even here. A young couple push a pram and carry the baby because the pram is full of flowers. The sun is coming down with the relentlessness of a thing that is about to burn out and I turn my face towards it. Teenagers kiss underneath a magnolia tree outside a church, which has columns that look like soft-serve ice cream. Children are on their way home from school. A small boy with a brown bowl cut is so serious. He has his hands in his pockets. He stops to tie his shoe-laces and I think he must have just been taught how to do that. When we walk past your old school, I feel like crying. All of the beginnings, all over the place. I can imagine you, a serious little boy. You must've kicked the ball, the way those boys in the field are doing. You must've trudged home and stopped to tie your shoe. I am happy even for these brick walls because you will have dragged a hand against them. I am so glad that the world has had a chance to be with you for a quarter of a century. My father used to say to my mother,

I like it when my roses see you.

The air smells of grass, dried out, and pools of cold water. You are walking home, with me. Hands in your pockets. A serious look on your face. Sometimes, it still feels like the beginning. I watch you squatting down to move a snail off the path and into a patch of grass. I have never met anyone as determined to be good as you. You coming over, one of the first times. Your hands shaking. It was surreal, watching you peel your shirt over your shoulders. Running my tongue along your waistband and feeling from the way that your stomach muscles tightened that you had tilted your head all the way back. It is still surreal. Calling your name and hearing you answer. Look at me. I am a teenage fool, writing you a note. Do you like me?

Tick yes or no. If yes, make me a ring out of dog roses. Make it always June. Make it always feel like the very beginning.

You bought me a book right at the start. You wrote in it,

To having our cake and eating it too.

This is a love story. The beginning and the end are the same, remember? No one will know what our marriage is like, if it happens. The story ends when I say yes or no. Or when you say no, after you've read this and realise that all the demons running through our woods look exactly like me. The same hair, flashing like fool's gold in a shaded creek.

When we get back to the apartment, we sit on the couch. You hold my hand, spin the ring around my finger.
    You say,
    Tell me a story. Tell me something nice.

And I say,
    Here's how it goes.

Once upon a time, a girl and a boy fell in love.

Acknowledgements

Thank you to my editors, Mary-Anne Harrington and Alison Callahan; the novel became so much better everytime you both shaped it. Thank you for your patience and vision.

Thank you to Chris Wellbelove for his support and for gently suggesting we give the readers a little bit of plot, as a treat. Thank you to Emily Fish for championing HERO so early on its journey. Thank you to the team at Aitken Alexander.

Thank you to the team at Tinder Press, with particular thanks to Ellie Freedman, Amy Cox, Yvonne Holland, Kate Truman, Joe Thomas, Alexia Thomaidis, Rabeeah Moeen, Tina Paul and Inka Melson. Thank you to Taylor Rondestvedt and the wider team at Scout Press; Jennifer Long, Laura Levatino, Aimee Bell, Caroline Pallotta, John P Jones, Jennifer Bergstrom, and Lisa Litwack.

I am very grateful to Gill and Rod Giddins, Claire Berliner, Halle O'Neal, Christina Carè, Tom Conaghan, Ella Baron, Niamh Hunt, Beth Alliband, Phil White, Rachel Chisholm, Lavinia Greenlaw, Matt Thorne, Anna Whitwham, Nick Ristic, Chisato Shiraishi, Ellie Roppolo, Megan Girdwood, Oswaldo Maciá, Anne Lise Kjaer and Harald Brekke for their support and encouragement.

Thank you to Francesa Taiganides, Zoë Fillingham and Isabel Madau-Martin. I love you all very much.

Thank you to Elizabeth Krupa for letting me sleep in your bed when we were little and for Phoebe and Maybelle. Thank you to Susan Buckley for many things, not least filling my life with books.

And thank you to Vicente, for everything.